Hello Kitty
GUIDE TO LONDON

Discover Hello Kitty's top sights!

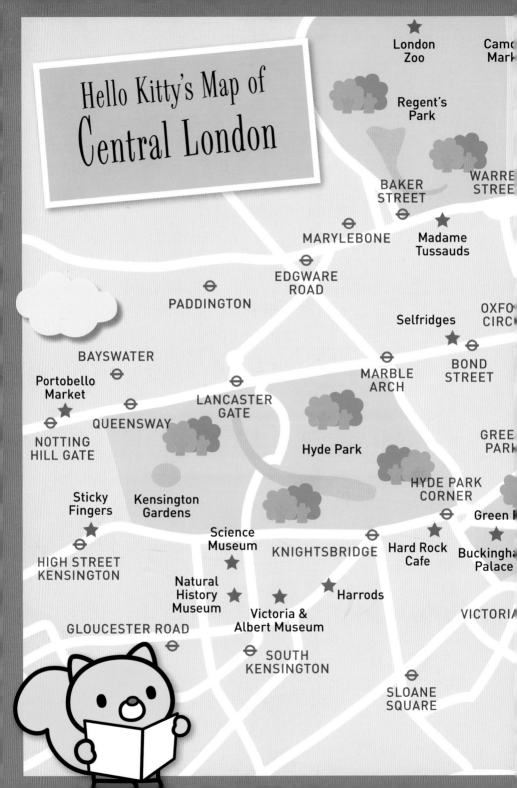

Hello Kitty's Map of Central London

London Zoo

Cam Mark

Regent's Park

WARRE STREE

BAKER STREET

MARYLEBONE

Madame Tussauds

EDGWARE ROAD

PADDINGTON

Selfridges

OXFO CIRC

BAYSWATER

MARBLE ARCH

BOND STREET

Portobello Market

LANCASTER GATE

QUEENSWAY

NOTTING HILL GATE

Hyde Park

GREE PARK

Sticky Fingers

Kensington Gardens

HYDE PARK CORNER

Green

Science Museum

KNIGHTSBRIDGE

Hard Rock Cafe

Buckingha Palace

HIGH STREET KENSINGTON

Natural History Museum

Harrods

VICTORIA

Victoria & Albert Museum

GLOUCESTER ROAD

SOUTH KENSINGTON

SLOANE SQUARE

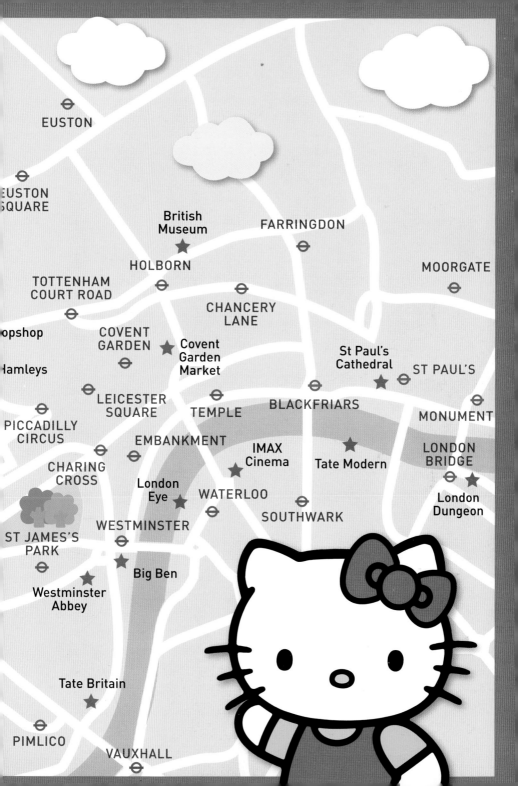

First published in the UK by HarperCollins Children's Books in 2012
1 3 5 7 9 10 8 6 4 2
ISBN: 978-0-00-746721-1

Written by Kirsty Neale

www.harpercollins.co.uk
Printed and bound in China

Hello Kitty

GUIDE TO LONDON

Discover Hello Kitty's top sights!

HarperCollins *Children's Books*

Welcome to my
Guide to London

I love living in London, it's such a fantastic town – big, noisy and full of some of the most super-fabulous people in the world. It really is one of the most amazing cities.

Not only is it a historical city, London is also a royal city, a theatrical city, a fashionable city and a working city, so no wonder it's such a great place to explore. Wherever you go, there are lots and lots of exciting and oh-so-super-stylish things to do. For example, did you know you can actually sleepover at the Science Museum? Or that you can watch a Puppet Show on a barge on the Thames? Or even that you can travel across London by duck? There really is so much to do! And I can't wait to share it all with you!

That's why I've packed this book full of my favourite places, brilliant insider information, fantastic shopping secrets plus wonderful things to

look out for. I've made sure everything's as up to date as possible, but it's always a really good idea to ring and double-check before you go.
Oh, and don't forget to consult a map when you're planning your visit, so you can see which sights are close to (and far away from!), each other!

Whether you are a new arrival, a visitor, or just someone who wants to read about London, I hope this book gives you some idea of all the fabulous things that London has in store for you. And whatever you get up to, make sure you have fun and enjoy your time in London.

Lots of love

Hello Kitty
x x

See the Sights!

When I have friends who are only in London for a day or two, I usually take them on a sightseeing trip. It's a really good way to whizz around town and see as much as possible, from the famous bits of the city, to some brilliant views and snippets of everyday London. There are lots of different types of sightseeing trip, and you can find some of them listed over the next few pages.

London Bus Tours

London bus tours are probably the most popular way to see the sights. Most of them work as 'hop-on, hop-off' trips. You buy a ticket at the start of the day, and can get on and off the bus as often as you like. This is great because you don't necessarily have to do much planning ahead. If you feel like taking a closer look at Buckingham Palace or Tower Bridge, you can just jump off at the nearest bus stop and check it out. It doesn't matter if you spend a few hours looking round, or just a few minutes – you can get back on to the bus again whenever you like.

I'd like to do this ☐

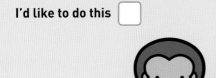

On Your Bike!

Touring London on a bicycle is a different – and very cool – way to go sightseeing! You don't need to worry about having or finding your own bicycle. The tour usually includes hiring a bike as well. It's quite important that you're confident and happy cycling. The guides are brilliant at taking you along the safest routes and quietest backstreets, but it's still not like going for a ride in the countryside! I don't cycle in London very often, but I feel much safer doing it with a group of other people. Some of the routes also include lots of cycling through parks, and those are usually the ones I look out for.

When you're on the tour, the guide will stop to talk to you about the sights as you reach them. As well as meaning you don't have to listen and concentrate on riding at the same time, this also gives you short breaks all the way along the route. Tours mostly go at a fairly slow pace, but they are quite long.

I'd like to do this

Cycling through Hyde Park

Captain Kidd's Canary Wharf Voyage

Hold on tight! This fantastic voyage is probably London's speediest sightseeing trip. A super-fast speedboat whizzes you along the river, from the London Eye to Canary Wharf and back again in less than an hour. You'll get to see plenty of sights and London landmarks, including St Paul's Cathedral, Big Ben and the Globe Theatre. The boat also passes right underneath Tower Bridge twice – once on the way downriver, and again on the way back!

The guides on board are specially trained to fit as much information as possible into the tour, so you're not missing out on a single thing. Although it's speedy, the boat travels further than most river cruises, so there's a lot to look at.

Insider tip!
The tour guides are actually professional stand-up comedians with a whole host of awards under their super-entertaining belts! They are guaranteed to have you in stitches!

I'd like to do this

Duck Tours

Not sure whether you want to go on a bus tour or a river trip? A Duck Tour is a little bit of both! Ducks, or DUKWs, are amphibious landing vehicles, which is just a fancy way of saying they're a type of bus that works on land and water. They were originally used during World War Two to carry troops ashore, but they're now one of the coolest ways to take a tour of London.

The bright yellow Ducks set off on land, near to the London Eye, and take you past landmarks including Big Ben, Trafalgar Square, Buckingham Palace and Westminster Abbey. You then switch from land to water – my favourite part of the tour. Slipping down a ramp and splashing into the river is an amazing feeling, and something you only get on a Duck!

I'd like to do this ☐

Insider tip!
It's a good idea to try and book your tickets in advance. Tours run every 30-60 minutes during the day, but there are only 30 seats on each bus.

Harry Potter walk

London Walks

London walks, or walking tours, are a very particular type of sightseeing. Instead of visiting the best-known sights and landmarks, they're usually based on a special subject. The tour then takes you to places that are linked to that subject in some way. For instance, a tour with a Halloween theme might lead you past haunted buildings or to spots where ghosts have been seen.

Walking tours often tend to be a mixture of storytelling and history, rather than lots of facts and figures. You can find tours on all kinds of subjects, including celebrities, spies, the 1960s, the Romans, Victorian London, *Doctor Who* and royal weddings. One of my favourites is a Harry Potter tour. I love taking my magic-loving pals on a walk that shows them lots of London, but also some of the real-life settings from their favourite movies!

I'd like to do this ☐

The Ghost Bus

All aboard the Fright Bus, for the scariest tour in town! This spooksome double-decker stands out even in London traffic because it's painted deepest, darkest black. And according to the creepy conductor, it's also haunted...

Setting off after dark, the Ghost Bus takes you on a ride round the grizzly history of London. You'll learn about the ghoulish graveyards, hear sinister stories and drive past the city's most haunted buildings.

I probably shouldn't tell you this, but the conductor and his just-as-spooky sidekick are actually actors. Although the bus takes you on a proper sightseeing tour, it also works a bit like a theatre show. There are even flatscreen TVs and a sound system on the bus to add some technical trickery and a sinister soundtrack to your trip.

The tour lasts for about an hour and 15 minutes, and as well as being lots of fun, it's a brilliant way to see London at night.

I'd like to do this ☐

Look out for!
My favourite bits of the tour included a haunted theatre, the famous tale of Sweeney Todd and the very spooky story of a black dog. Eeek!

The London Eye

The London Eye is one of the most famous sights in the city. It's officially called an observation wheel, and is the tallest one in Europe. There are 32 glass capsules, known as pods, attached to the outside. Each one of these holds up to 25 people. Once you're inside, it's up to you if you want

to sit down on one of the benches in the middle or wander around. I much prefer standing up because you get to see loads more!

From the very top of the wheel, the view stretches out up to 25 miles in every direction. I love looking out for landmarks like St Paul's, Hyde Park (green spaces are easy to spot!), the Gherkin, the tall and skinny Post Office Tower and even Windsor Castle, way off in the distance.

Unlike Ferris wheels at fairs or theme parks, the London Eye moves really slowly. It takes about half an hour for your pod to make it all the way round, and because it's so slow, you can easily walk off while it's still moving.

It's also really fun to visit the London Eye in the evening. You'll get a very different view, and even rain can't stop London looking beautiful when it's lit up after dark!

I'd like to do this

Did you know?
You don't 'ride' on the London Eye – you go on a 'flight'.

The Monument

The Monument is the tallest and oldest single stone column in the world. It was built to commemorate the Great Fire of London in 1666, and although it's not easy to see from the ground, the shiny bit on the top is actually a pot full of golden flames. From start to finish, it took six years to build, and is 202 feet (about 61 metres) tall. If you could lie the Monument on its side, it would reach exactly as far as the spot where the Great Fire started, 202 feet away in a bakery on Pudding Lane.

So, why am I getting all excited about a giant stone column? Because you can walk up to the top and look out over London! Inside, there's a spiral staircase with 311 steps. They're really narrow and winding, but it's totally worth it for the view at the top. My favourite part was seeing Tower Bridge, but I also loved the fun, talking telescopes, which tell you exactly what you're looking at all the way round.

I'd like to go here

Insider tip!
Don't visit the Monument thinking you can be lazy and take a lift to the top – there isn't one! But if you manage to climb all the way to the top and back down again, you get a cool certificate to prove it.

Kensington Palace

Kensington Palace has been home to members of the royal family for around 400 years. Queen Victoria was born in the palace, and Princes William and Harry grew up there too. Even though some of the palace is open to the public now, quite a few royals still live in other parts of the building. I've never bumped into one yet, but it's fun to think they might be hanging out somewhere nearby!

The parts of the palace you do get to have a good look at are still pretty cool. There's Queen Victoria's bedroom, the pretty sunken gardens, the staterooms, the King's picture gallery and an amazing staircase where the walls and ceiling are covered in lifelike paintings. I always look forward to having posh tea and cakes in the Orangery before I go home too!

I'd like to go here

Look out for!

Kensington Gardens is just behind the palace. It's got a huge pond, a fancy water-garden, and famous statues of Prince Albert (Queen Victoria's husband) and Peter Pan!

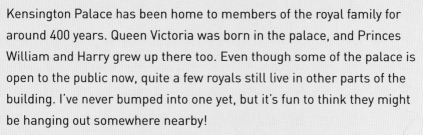

Trafalgar Square

Trafalgar Square is one of the first places I take my friends when they come to visit London. They've usually seen it on TV or in films, but it's even better in person. Right in the middle is Nelson's Column, which is a super-huge 51 metres high, and there are lots of other statues around the square. The fountains in the middle are guarded by four big bronze lions, which make a brilliant photo opportunity. You're not supposed to climb on to them, so we always try and snap some pics sitting between their paws!

The square used to be famous for its flock of around 35,000 pigeons. People fed them seeds and bits of leftover food, but they made the square really dirty. It's now against the law to feed them, and birds of prey are flown in the square by special handlers to keep the pigeons away.

I'd like to go here

Did you know?
When you see a road sign saying 'London, 10 miles' (or any number of miles) the distance is always measured from Trafalgar Square.

Kew Gardens

The Royal Botanic Gardens at Kew, in south-west London, is the world's biggest collection of living plants. As well as the gardens, it has six fabulous glasshouses, a library, a museum and a small royal palace. It's an amazing place if you're interested in nature, but you definitely don't need to know much about plants or gardens to have a brilliant time!

There are all sorts of gardens, including a pretty rose garden and one especially for bees. The glasshouses are all different too. I loved the underwater plants in the basement of the Palm House, and also the Evolution House, which is all about the history of plants, from the time of the dinosaurs, right up to today.

There's also a handy land-train, The Kew Explorer, which allows you to get round the huge gardens more quickly and easily.

My favourite part of the whole visit was the Rhizotron and Treetop Walkway. The Rhizotron is an underground display, where you can explore the roots of some giant trees. Then, when you've finished looking around, you climb straight up to the Walkway to see the trees from a completely different angle!

I'd like to go here

The Tower of London

The Tower of London is an ancient castle on the north bank of the river Thames. Since it was built over 900 years ago, it's mostly been used as a prison and a royal palace. Today, it's home to the Yeoman Warders, their famous black ravens and – my super-sparkly favourite part – the crown jewels!

As well as being a tourist attraction themselves, the Yeoman Warders act as brilliant tour guides around the Tower. They can fill you in on all sorts of grisly-but-interesting stories, including which important people were held in the prison here and who arrived through the watery Traitor's Gate. I especially loved finding out about the Royal Menagerie, a zoo with elephants, tigers, ostriches and kangaroos, all living inside the Tower.

In the White Tower, I got to see bits of graffiti carved into the wall by prisoners over 500 years ago, and outside on Tower Green, I stood on the exact spot where Anne Boleyn (one of King Henry VIII's wives) had her head chopped off. Eeek!

I'd like to go here

Look out for!
The Crown Jewels are truly fabulous. There are over 23,000 gems, including sapphires, emeralds, rubies, pearls and the world's biggest cut diamond.

Buckingham Palace and the Royal Mews

Buckingham Palace is the Queen's official home in London. It was built over 300 years ago, and has 775 rooms. Over 800 people work at the palace, which has its own post office, swimming pool, cinema, café and doctor's surgery. There's also a helicopter landing pad in the garden!

Every year, when the Queen heads off to Scotland on her holidays, some parts of the palace open up to the public. If you're lucky enough to get a ticket, you can have a good nosy around the grand staterooms, the super-fabulous ballroom and the palace gardens!

Royal Mews

The Royal Mews at Buckingham Palace is a busy, working stables. It's open to the public most days, although if the horses are busy training, you might not always get to see them when you visit. What you will see is the Queen's amazing collection of cars and horse-drawn carriages. They're used for official royal visits and special occasions, including royal weddings. My favourite was the super-glamorous gold State Coach. It's so shiny, I needed to wear sunglasses!

Changing the Guard

This ceremony happens in front of the palace, every day during the summer and every other day in winter. It lasts about 45 minutes and you can watch it for free from outside the palace gates. A military band plays different kinds of music during the ceremony, from marching songs and pop tunes, to *Happy Birthday* if one of the royals is celebrating.

I'd like to go here

Insider tip!
Check the flagpole on top of the palace to find out whether the Queen is at home or not. If the Royal Standard flag (red, yellow and blue) is flying, she's there, but if it's a red, white and blue Union flag, she's out.

HMS Belfast

HMS Belfast is a museum ship, floating on the River Thames between London Bridge and Tower Bridge. It's got an amazing history, and is especially important as the last surviving warship of its kind.

Once you arrive on board, there are nine floors to explore. I borrowed an audio guide to find my way around and get loads of extra info, but you can also follow the arrows on the floor. One of the coolest things about the guide was listening to stories told by some of the sailors who served on the ship. Up to 950 of them went on each mission and walking around HMS Belfast gives you an idea of what life at sea might have been like.

As well as the grand Captain's Bridge, the Wheelhouse and the cramped Engine and Boiler Rooms, you can also see some of the places ordinary sailors spent most of their time, including living quarters, the mess (where they ate) and the sickbay.

I'd like to go here

Look out for!
There are lots of hands-on activities on the ship. My favourite was getting to try on an original sailor's uniform!

Totally shipshape!

Leicester Square

Leicester Square is in the West End, between Trafalgar Square, Piccadilly Circus and Covent Garden. It's one of the busiest spots in London, especially at night. The square has been well known for entertainment since the 1800s, when it was lined with Turkish Baths, music halls and fancy restaurants. Now, it's in the middle of London's exciting cinema and theatreland, and often hosts big, important film premieres. Altogether, there are five cinemas on the square, plus three more nearby. I especially love wandering past the biggest one (Odeon Leicester Square) and looking down at the ground. Some bits of the pavement have been replaced by metal plaques to celebrate different films or events, and lots of them include the handprints of famous film stars. It's great fun bending down to see how the famous hands compare to your own!

As well as the cinemas, Leicester Square is also home to lots of pavement cafés, street artists and buskers. Each winter, a fair is set up in the square, and it often holds events as part of London's Chinese New Year celebrations too.

Insider tip!
Check the Internet to find out if any movie premieres are happening while you're in London. You might not be on the guest list, but anyone can stand in Leicester Square to watch the stars arrive and walk down the red carpet!

I'd like to go here

The Gherkin

The Gherkin is a skyscraper in the middle of the City. It's only been around since 2003, but is already an easy-to-spot and pretty cool part of the London skyline. Nicknamed 'Gherkin' because of its curvy shape, the building is officially called 30 St Mary Axe. I think the Gherkin is much more fun though, and most other people – even on TV and in the newspapers – seem to agree!

The building is 40 floors high and a whopping 180m tall. The sides are made from thousands of triangle-shaped panes of glass that you can easily see if you look closely. Believe it or not, there's only one single pane of curved glass in the whole building – the round 'lens' on the very top. The rest are all completely flat!

I'd like to go here

The Old Curiosity Shop

The Old Curiosity Shop was built in the 1500s, believe it or not. It's one of only a few buildings to survive The Great Fire of London and the Blitz during World War Two. Squashed between lots of bigger, taller buildings the tiny shop looks a bit like a doll's house! Even though I know it's there, it's always a surprise to walk round the corner and see something so ancient near all the traffic and busyness of modern London.

Inside, the floorboards are wonky, and the sloping roof is made from ancient wooden beams. Over the years, it's sold all sorts of things and was once even a dairy. At the moment, it's a fancy shoe shop, but it might be something completely different when you visit!

I'd like to go here

Westminster Abbey

Westminster Abbey, near the Houses of Parliament, is over 900 years old. It's the place where kings and queens of England have been crowned since 1066, and also where many of them are buried. Sixteen members of the royal family have got married in the Abbey, including the Queen and, in 2011, Prince William.

It's not just a place for royalty, though – there are memorials to soldiers, musicians and scientists in the Abbey, plus lots of writers buried in the famous Poet's Corner.

I've been to Westminster Abbey a couple of times, and it's much more interesting with a guided tour. You can either use a free audio guide (which is brilliant) or pay a bit extra if you'd prefer a real person! The guide takes you round the Abbey itself, and then there's a museum in the grounds and the Abbey Gardens to visit. These are really pretty, and

I especially liked the Infirmary Garden, which was used to grow herbs, fruit and veggies for making medicine. The poor head gardener only had one day off each year, so it must have been pretty important to stay healthy so he could enjoy it!

The Abbey still holds church services every day. Visiting times are set around these, and they're quite strict! Check the website to make sure you don't turn up at the wrong time.

I'd like to go here

Big Ben and The Houses of Parliament

The Houses of Parliament, which are also known as the Palace of Westminster, are the home of the British government. They were first built as a royal palace around 1,000 years ago, but lots of bits have been added or rebuilt since then.

On a guided tour, you get to visit a really good mixture of the old and new parts of the building, as well as finding out just what goes on inside. The building has nearly 1,200 rooms, 100 staircases and two miles of corridors, so there's plenty to see and discover!

Big Ben

Big Ben is the nickname for the bell inside the clock tower at the Houses of Parliament. Although that's what you hear chiming every hour, most people use the name 'Big Ben' for the whole clock. It's been keeping time in London for over 150 years, and has faces on all four sides of the tower. Each one lights up at night so you can still see the time clearly and easily.

I'd like to go here

Timing Tip!
Although you can visit the Houses of Parliament at any time of year, guided tours are only available on Saturdays and during the summer. They get quite busy, so it's a good idea to book in advance if you can.

Piccadilly Circus

Piccadilly Circus is right in the heart of the West End. It's a bit like a giant roundabout and is always bustling with traffic and pedestrians. Lots of people use it as a meeting place, and you've probably seen the famous video screens and brightly lit signs on TV or in films. It's surrounded by huge buildings, including a theatre and a smart shopping arcade.

A little way away from the traffic, the Shaftesbury Memorial Fountain is another famous London landmark. If you don't recognise the name, don't worry – I had to look it up too! Most people call it 'Eros' after the arrow-shooting statue on the top.

I love visiting Piccadilly in the evening, when the lights make it look really amazing. The last time I went to see a show at one of the theatres on Shaftesbury Avenue, I walked from Piccadilly Circus, and it really started the evening in style!

The Ritz

The Ritz Hotel is a short walk along Piccadilly (the street, not the Circus!). It's beautiful and super-grand inside, but still worth admiring from the outside, even if you're not staying there or going for afternoon tea. If you are lucky enough to have tea at the super-stylish Ritz, make sure you dress up – there's a strict dress code.

I'd like to go here ☐

Tower Bridge Exhibition

Tower Bridge crosses the River Thames near the Tower of London. It was opened in 1894, and the Victorians nicknamed it the Wonder Bridge. One of the most impressive things about the bridge is the giant moveable roadway between the two towers. Each side lifts up so that tall ships can

pass underneath. There are barriers on either side to stop the traffic before the road begins to lift.

The Tower Bridge Exhibition lets you explore the bridge even more closely. It includes special video clips and interactive displays on how it was built and how it works. As well as going down into the Victorian Engine Rooms, you also get to catch a lift up to the high-level walkways – my favourite bit of the exhibition! The walkways are 42 metres above the river, which means you get a pretty amazing view. As you walk across, there are special windows every so often, just so you can stop and take photographs. Don't forget to snap a few extras when you get back down to street level, so you can show everyone exactly where you were standing when you took those amazing high-up snaps of the river!

I'd like to go here ☐

Timing Tip!
The bridge is raised around 1,000 times a year to let ships pass along the river. If you want to watch it happening, you can find out the exact dates and times on the Tower Bridge website.

Hampton Court Palace and Maze

Hampton Court Palace is in south-west London. It's most famous as the home of King Henry VIII, although many other people, including Elizabeth I, have lived there too. When you visit the Palace, you might even catch sight of some of them, as there are lots of rumours about ghosts and hauntings!

As well as spooks, you can also explore the Tudor Great Hall, the Queen's State Apartments, the King's Apartments, the super-impressive gardens and the palace kitchens. These were one of the busiest bits of the Palace, and during King Henry's time they fed 600 people, twice a day.

The Maze

The maze is my favourite part of Hampton Court. Planted in around 1700, it's one of the oldest surviving hedge mazes in the world. It has lots of twists, turns and dead ends to confuse people as they follow the path to the middle. It usually takes around 20 minutes to solve, although I'm pretty sure I was lost for much longer than that!

I'd like to go here ☐

31

London Girls Just Want to Have Fun!

There are so many fun things to do in London, it's sometimes hard to know where to start! That's why I've gathered some of my very favourite activities here especially for you. Whether you fancy arriving at London Zoo by a super-special canal entrance, walking underneath the Thames, or horse-riding through a park, you'll find endlessly exciting things to do in this section.

London Zoo

London Zoo in Regent's Park is the oldest scientific zoo in the world. It opened over 180 years ago, and is now home to more than 16,000 animals. The zoo is divided up into different areas, and the creatures all live in enclosures that are as close as possible to their natural habitat. As well as making the animals happier, this makes the zoo even more amazing for visitors. You can walk through a real, living rainforest, head off to Penguin Beach, or climb up on to a special treetop viewing platform and find yourself eye to eye with a giraffe!

I loved visiting Butterfly Paradise, where moths and butterflies are free to fly all around you, and Happy Families, which is full of super-cute otters, lemurs and meerkats. Wherever you go, the animal keepers are happy to chat and answer any questions. You can watch as they feed the

Did you know?
The money you pay to visit London Zoo isn't just used to take care of the creatures that live there. The zoo also helps to save animals from extinction all over the world.

animals, and there might even be a chance for you to help out, if you're really lucky. There was more than enough to keep me busy for a whole day, from the sweetest little monkeys to sleek and chic zebras, but what was my favourite thing? The Big Cats exhibit, no competition!

I'd like to go here

Namco Funscape

Namco Funscape is in the County Hall building, just next to the London Eye. It's one of the biggest amusement arcades in London, with lots of things to do over three different floors. Most things inside take the Funscape's own currency, the Nam, instead of real coins. So, after swapping my pocket money for a handful of Nam, I headed for the video games, which are amazing. There are over 200 different kinds to choose from, including virtual horse-racing, skateboarding and cyber-cycling. My favourite was the downhill skiing, which was much warmer than real skiing, although without the cute snow-boots!

As well as the virtual games, there are quite a few real ones. You can go Techno-Bowling, where the lanes are lit with ultraviolet lights (so cool!), or try racing around in the turbo-charged bumper cars.

If all that excitement gets a bit too much, there's also a lounge area full of squashy sofas and giant TV screens, where you can grab something to eat.

I'd like to go here

Look out for!
NAMOKE is Namco's super-cool version of karaoke. Shut yourself and your family or friends into a private room, pick your tunes from the touch-screen selection and grab a microphone.

Canal Boat Trip

The Regent's Canal runs between Little Venice and Camden Lock. A boat trip along the canal takes around 45 minutes in each direction, and you'll get to see some really interesting and unusual bits of London along the way. From fancy bridges to ever-so-slightly spooky tunnels, there are also grand houses and canal-side gardens to see along the route. Some parts take you through the edges of Regent's Park, and I spotted a few sneak peeks of the zoo as we floated past too.

There are a couple of different boat services you can use, and one of them even lets you hop off halfway to use their special canal entrance right into the zoo itself. Talk about arriving in style!

I travelled on a pretty, painted narrowboat, which made for a cute photo-opportunity, as well as a fun trip. We finished the journey at Camden Lock, with plenty of time (and shopping bags!) to explore the famous market.

I'd like to do this ☐

Insider tip!

At the start of the tour, everyone gets kitted out with a life jacket. You can also borrow waterproofs and wet-weather clothes if it's raining, or if you're worried about getting splashed!

Messing about on the river!

35

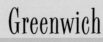

Greenwich is one of my favourite parts of London. It's a great place to go for a day out because there's so much to do there, and lots of variety. I've made you a list of things to do and places to visit. Have fun!

Greenwich Market is completely fabulous! It's mostly undercover, which means you can shop in comfort even when it's raining. There are over 100 stalls, crammed full of art, crafts, fashion, jewellery and yummy fresh food. It's not open on Mondays, and there are different stalls on different days. Check out the website to see what's going on before you visit.

Boat Trips leave Greenwich at least twice an hour during the summer, going in both directions. On a cruise boat, you head along the river, seeing the sights as a tour guide points out all the most interesting bits. You can also catch Thames Clipper boats here, if you're heading back into the middle of town and don't want to use the trains or buses.

The Fan Museum is small but super-pretty! It has a collection of over 3,500 fans, and is the only museum of its kind anywhere in the world.

Time is measured from Greenwich, which makes it the official starting point of each new day and year! You can see the exact point (the Prime Meridian) at the **Royal Observatory**. As well as time, the observatory lets you explore space. The daily planetarium shows are amazing. They include info from NASA telescopes, and you can also try your hand at being an astronaut or guiding a space mission.

Greenwich Foot Tunnel runs underneath the river to the Isle of Dogs on the other side. Look out for the glass-domed entrance in Cutty Sark Gardens, if you want to try this fun way of getting across the Thames.

Make sure you leave time to hang out in **Greenwich Park** for a while. It has a boating lake, a deer enclosure and even an apple orchard! Some of the park is on quite a steep slope, but it's worth climbing up just for the amazing view of London. I always make sure to take my camera so I can snap some pics of the city as a reminder of my day out.

I'd like to go here

Madame Tussauds

Madame Tussauds is one of London's best-known museums. Full of life-sized figures made from wax, you've probably never seen a bigger – or stranger – collection of famous faces all in the same place. I had my photo taken with Prince William, asked Johnny Depp for some acting tips and even managed to track down the Invisible Woman!

The museum is split into separate sections, and each one has a different theme. As well as the Movie Room, Sports Zone and Music Megastars, there are waxworks of famous artists, writers, scientists, world leaders and royals from throughout history. My favourite part was the A-List Party room, which makes you feel like you've sneaked into a glitzy, showbiz bash! There are celebrity figures everywhere, so you might find yourself bumping into David and Victoria Beckham one minute and posing with a supermodel the next.

I also liked The Spirit of London, which is a special ride inside the museum. It takes you on a trip through the history of London, from the Tudors to the 1980s, via things like the Great Fire of London and the Swinging Sixties. It's a crazy-but-brilliant mixture of people and events, pretty much like everything else in Madame Tussauds!

I'd like to go here

I heart nature!

London Wetlands Centre

The London Wetlands Centre is one of the best places to watch city wildlife in the whole of Europe. There are so many rare creatures to be spotted that expert scientists come to study and visit them alongside normal tourists like you and me!

The centre is pretty huge, with large lakes, smaller ponds, meadows and woods. There are walkways round most of these, and also plenty of hides – tiny huts where you can sit and watch through a window to get an even closer view. Lots of birds and animals are quite shy of people, so keeping yourself out of sight in one of these often means you get to see more.

If you're not sure what to look out for, it's a good idea to go on one of the free guided walks. These are led by wildlife wardens, who will sometimes let you help out with feeding the animals too. I spotted all kinds of different birds, including some bright green parakeets, as well as ducks, swans, frogs, lizards, bats, dragonflies, butterflies and a couple of super-cute, furry water voles!

Look out for!
The centre often holds special events and activities. I had a go at pond dipping, visited the Bat House and also learned how to forage for plants and berries to eat.

I'd like to go here

Sporting Tours

From the Olympic Park to the Oval cricket ground, London has lots of famous sporting venues. Many of them – including Wembley Stadium and the Wimbledon Lawn Tennis Club – offer tours, even if you can't go to an actual match, game or event.

Wembley Stadium

Wembley is one of the most famous stadiums in the world. As well as football and sports events, it's also used to stage enormous rock concerts. It has a whopping 90,000 seats, and although I didn't have time to try out all of them, it was fun exploring all the best views and snapping some cool photos!

The stadium tour takes you behind the scenes to visit the England football team changing rooms, the press room and the royal box. You also get the chance to follow in the footsteps of your heroes – whether they're footballers or musicians – and walk out on to the pitch through the players' tunnel.

Wimbledon

Wimbledon is the world's oldest tennis tournament. It's the only one of the four Grand Slam championships to be played on grass. The Wimbledon Lawn Tennis Club tour gives you VIP access to explore behind the scenes. The route of the tour varies, depending on what's happening at the club, but I got to see Centre Court (which was super-exciting!),

Court No.1, the Picnic Terraces and the BBC Television Studio. We also sneaked a look at the press room, where players are interviewed after big matches, whether they've won or lost.

Your tour ticket also lets you visit the Wimbledon Lawn Tennis Museum, where cool interactive touch screens help you explore the history of the game.

I'd like to go here

BFI Imax Cinema

If you're anywhere nearby, it's pretty hard to miss the IMAX cinema on the South Bank. It's a huge, circular building that shoots up from the middle of a roundabout, right at the end of Waterloo Bridge.

Want some facts and figures? The screen is taller than five double-decker buses and wider than six. It's the biggest in the whole of the UK, and there's room for almost 500 people to sit and watch each film!

Although they show lots of big new movies, there are also smaller films on all kinds of subjects. Most of these are in super-cool 3D, which means you get to sit and watch them wearing a pair of special – and enormous! – glasses. I've seen 3D movies about space, lions, dinosaurs and dolphins, as well as a couple of Disney and Harry Potter films. With such a huge screen, and loud surround-sound too, you almost feel like you're in the film, which is pretty amazing! It's not like going to a normal cinema, although don't worry – they still have popcorn and pic'n'mix for you to scoff as you watch.

I'd like to go here

London Parks

I love hanging out at the park, and not just when it's warm in the spring and summer. Parks look super-pretty when the leaves change colour in autumn, and are brilliant for snowball fights or frosty walks in winter too!

Parklife!

Regent's Park is one of London's Royal Parks. The best-known part is probably London Zoo, but there are plenty of other things too. If you're feeling sporty, there are tennis courts and a boating lake, where you can hire rowing or pedal boats. I love the pretty wildlife garden and the cool timber treehouse. It's also fun to rent a deckchair and hang out near one of the bandstands where you can listen to free music. There's also a fabulous open-air theatre.

St. James's Park is surrounded by palaces! There's St. James's Palace, the Queen's home Buckingham Palace and the Palace of Westminster, otherwise known as the Houses of Parliament. The bridge over the lake is the perfect spot to snap a photo of Buckingham Palace, and has a great view of the London Eye. Make your way to Duck Island at around 2.30 in the afternoon if you want to see the pelicans being fed their fishy lunch!

Hyde Park is right next to Kensington Gardens, and the Serpentine (a huge lake) runs through the middle. It's the perfect place to walk, cycle or roller-skate, and you can also play tennis or visit the Serpentine Art Gallery. I love checking out the world-famous Speaker's Corner, where you can stand up and make a public speech about anything you like. Even if you're too shy to speak, it's fun to listen to other people! In the summer there are often free band concerts, and right in the centre of the park, you'll find a gorgeous meadow with wildflowers, birds and butterflies. Oh, and look out for the very strange Upside Down Tree!

Holland Park is brilliant. It's got squirrels, peacocks, a giant chess set, an adventure playground and its own waterfall! The park used to be the garden of a grand mansion house, but most of the building was destroyed during the war. The ruins are used as the backdrop for plays performed by the Holland Park Open Air Theatre.

Crystal Palace Park is also amazing. As well as the eerie ruins of the Crystal Palace (a giant, glass exhibition hall), the park has three lakes, a concert bowl and a super-fun maze. There's loads of room to spread out and have a picnic, or if you don't feel like feeding yourself, there's a small farm where the animals will eat snacks right out of your hand. The best bit, though, is the dinosaurs. Seriously – it's a park with dinosaurs! They were part of the original Crystal Palace exhibition, and you can still see them lurking between the trees and around the edges of the boating lake now.

Richmond Park was originally a deer park, and more than 600 red and fallow deer still live there. If you visit in autumn, you might get to see some of the male deer fighting, or rutting – roaring and clashing their antlers together. The deer aren't the park's only animals. I love looking out for the shire horses, Billy and Massey, who work there to help look after special areas of grassland. They're a bit like super-cute, sugar-lump-eating lawnmowers!

I'd like to go to . . . . **park!**

Hyde Park Riding Stables

How would you like to visit Hyde Park on four legs instead of two? Hyde Park Stables offer riders the chance to walk (or trot!) round the park on one of their specially-chosen horses. It doesn't matter whether you're a total beginner or a more experienced rider – all rides include lessons and tips to help you out.

When I visited, we learned a few basic skills first, and then set out from the stables in a group. It sounds incredible, but Hyde Park has five miles of bridle paths. Riding, learning and seeing the sights as we went along was very cool. I spotted lots of things I'd never noticed before, just because the view is so different from a horse!

I'd like to go here

Sea Life London Aquarium

The London Aquarium is another of the attractions in County Hall, just between Westminster Bridge and the London Eye. It's home to thousands of sea creatures from all over the world, including seahorses, stingrays, sharks, crocodiles, octopuses, piranhas, penguins and – of course – fish!

The aquarium is set out over three floors, and has 14 separate discovery zones. The newest of these is the Penguin Ice Adventure, where you can watch a super-cute family of Gentoo penguins splash, and learn about how they survive in the coldest place on earth. There's also a special ice cave with a window, that gives you a close-up view as the penguins splash, play and dive beneath the chilly water.

You can get just as close to lots of other animals in the aquarium, from crocodiles in the Rainforest Zone, to green turtles in the Tropical Ocean Tunnel. There are touch-pools all over the place, and if you've got the nerve, you should also check out the Shark Walk – a floating glass platform over a tank full of sharks. As you walk across, you can see four different types of shark swimming right under your feet. It's scary, but totally amazing too. I dare you to give it a go!

I'd like to go here

Look out for!
Feeding time! You can watch lots of the animals, including sharks, terrapins, penguins and rays being fed, and sometimes get the chance to help out too.

London Dungeon

A sign outside The London Dungeon says 'Enter at your peril', and if you're easily spooked, that's good advice! The Dungeon uses a mixture of rides, special effects and some very creepy actors to lead you through 2,000 years of horrible history. There are 14 different sections, and they're all dark and gloomy to add to the spookiness.

From Executioner's Corner to the Scary Surgery, I spent half of the visit jumping out of my skin!

But if you don't mind being a bit scared there's plenty of fun and silliness going on too. Me and my friends laughed just as much as we squealed on the way round. As well as the Surgery section, I also loved the Great Fire of London and the Traitor boat ride. It's not actually a real boat – it's more like a super-spooky ghost train with sticky cobwebs and lots of strange noises. If you decide to give it a go, make sure to watch out for the very scary chopping axe blade. Eek!

I'd like to go here

Look out for!
Some of the actors hide in gloomy corners and jump out when you're not expecting it. They also tell the best ghost stories I've ever heard!

the Dungeon
SHOP OF HORRORS

1 UNIQUE EXPERIENCE

14 ACTO... ...D SHOW...

Ripley's Believe It Or Not

Ripley's Believe It Or Not! on Piccadilly Circus is a museum crammed full of strange and amazing exhibits. Spread over five floors, it's based on the work of a man named Robert Ripley. He first displayed his collection of unusual items over 80 years ago, in a museum called The Odditorium. The idea was turned into a radio show, then a TV series and then back into a museum.

There's so much to see when you get inside, it's tricky to know where to start. From a painting on a grain of rice, to a model of Tower Bridge made from 264,345 matchsticks, I'm not sure I've ever said 'Wow' so many times in just a few hours! My favourite exhibit was a Mini car, covered in a million sparkly crystals. Like lots of the things in the museum, that probably seems unbelievable, but it's totally true – there are exactly one million crystals glued to the car!

A few of the exhibits are also interactive. I eventually found my way out of the amazing Mirror Maze, and got even dizzier trying to make it through the Spinning Tunnel. There's a special museum camera that snaps your photo near the end of the tunnel, so make sure you smile, unless you want to look as cross-eyed and wobbly as I did!

I'd like to go here

BBC Tour

Take a tour of the world-famous BBC TV Centre in west London and find out what really goes on behind the scenes of a television show! Nicknamed 'The Doughnut', TV Centre has been making programmes for over 50 years. It's still a busy, working building, which means the things you'll see on a tour are different each day.

When I went along, we visited the backstage green room area, the newsroom, the weather centre, one of the TV studios and even got to peek inside a dressing room. The public don't usually get to see any of these places, which made it even more exciting. I was a bit disappointed not to bump into any TV stars, but our guide said people taking the tour quite often get to spot a famous face or two on the way round!

Usually, when I go on trips and tours, my camera is the first thing I pack. Although you're allowed to take one into TV Centre, you can't use it everywhere. The tour guides always tell you when it's OK, and I was especially glad they did when we reached some

Timing Tip!
You have to book if you want to tour TV Centre, you can't just turn up on the day. That doesn't mean you need to plan your visit weeks or months in advance – sometimes just a few days is enough.

super-cool BBC props. I think having my photo taken standing next to Doctor Who's Tardis was my favourite part of the whole tour!

I'd like to go here

Skating Heaven

Skating Heaven is in east London. Their Family Skate event on Sunday afternoon is open to everyone, whether you're a skating sensation or a first-time roller.

When you arrive, they whisk you off to Skate Hire, where you can pick up skates, a helmet and protective gear to keep you safe. Then, if you're a beginner, it's straight to Boot Camp, which is honestly lots more fun than it sounds! The expert Boot Camp instructors teach you how to skate, or brush up your skills, with lots of fun activities and games. When you're done, you can choose whether to get sporty or head for the roller disco. The sporty stuff includes roller hockey, skate ball and roller basketball, which all sound cool, but for me the disco always wins!

There are loads of chances to do your own thing and see how your coolest moves work on wheels, but you also get to learn the Skating Heaven line dance. I love the fact it's easy enough for beginners to do, but still has plenty for my super-skater friends to enjoy too. The end of the session usually rolls round way too quickly for me, but I always look forward to joining in with the super-fun Skating Train before it's time to head home.

I'd like to go here

49

London Lidos

A lido is an outdoor public swimming pool. There are quite a few in London, and on a hot, sunny day, they're a fabulous place to hang out!

Tooting Bec Lido is the biggest outdoor swimming pool in England, and also one of the oldest. There's a nearby café and a grassy area for sunbathing or scoffing an after-swim picnic.

The Serpentine Lido in Hyde Park is actually a section of the Serpentine lake. If you're lucky, you might find yourself swimming alongside the park's ducks and swans! The lido isn't heated, which means it can be a brilliant way to cool down in the middle of summer.

Brockwell Lido, in Brockwell Park, is a short train journey away from Victoria Station. It's a big open-air pool, that has been popular with swimmers for over 70 years. People who live nearby sometimes call the lido 'Brixton Beach'!

Hampstead Heath Lido (also known as

Parliament Hill Lido) is one of four places to swim on the heath. There are also three bathing pools nearby – one for men, one for women and one for everyone to share!

I'd like to go to . . . . **Lido!**

The Vault, Hard Rock Café

The Vault below the Hard Rock Café Shop is a tiny treasure trove of music history. The building used to be a bank, and The Vault is in the room that was the bank's actual vault!

Free tours start every 20 minutes from the shop upstairs, and the guides will tell you about all the guitars, costumes and other bits of memorabilia on display. My favourite was one of Madonna's old credit cards!

I took loads of snaps as we looked around, and you can also have a special souvenir photo taken holding one of the rare guitars. My top tip? Pull your best popstar pose and totally rock out when they press the shutter!

Don't forget to have a good look round the shop upstairs afterwards. They sell lots of cool stuff, including T-shirts, caps, hoodies, games and books. I bought a badge to pin on my favourite jacket, and a few extras for my friends as fun souvenirs of our visit.

I'd like to go here

51

Warner Bros. Studio Tour London

The Making of Harry Potter tour at Leavesden Studios is your chance to peek behind the scenes of the magical movie series. All eight were filmed at Leavesden, and many of the sets, props and costumes are still there. As well as wandering through bits of Hogwarts (Dumbledore's Office and the Great Hall were my favourites!), you'll also find out how some of the clever special effects were made.

The two enormous Harry Potter 'stages' inside the studio are full of amazing things you'll recognise from the films. What's even cooler, though, is that you'll be able to see lots of little details the camera doesn't show. The sets look even bigger in real life than they do on screen, and it was exciting to walk in the footsteps of my favourite characters!

Insider tip!
Make sure you book! It takes 20-30 minutes to reach Leavesden from central London, and the tour itself lasts around three hours. You have to book in advance, so don't make the journey unless you've already got a ticket.

I'd like to go here

The London Brass Rubbing Centre

The London Brass Rubbing Centre is in the church of St Martin in the Fields on Trafalgar Square. You'll find it downstairs in the crypt, which isn't anywhere as creepy as it sounds.

Not sure what brass rubbing is? Don't worry – I didn't know either! Brasses are a kind of picture or plaque often found in old churches. By placing a piece of paper on top, and then rubbing over it with wax, you can make a cool copy of the picture underneath.

It only takes a few minutes to learn how to do it, and the people at the centre give you the paper and shimmery metallic wax you need to get started. They've got about 90 brasses for you to choose from, including pictures of fabulously dressed ladies, dashing knights, lions, unicorns and a very popular dragon. I picked an especially glam-looking lady, and in no time at all had an amazing piece of art to take home. There was even time to make a few extras to give away as presents!

Don't worry if you make a mistake – the super-smart staff have loads of tips on how to make them disappear.

I'd like to go here

Mudchute Park and Farm

Mudchute Park and Farm is in an area of east London known as the Isle of Dogs. It's London's biggest city farm, with over 200 animals, including cows, sheep, pigs, llamas, goats, chickens, ducks, horses, peacocks and a python!

Standing in the middle of a huge field with horses or cows when you can also see skyscrapers in the distance feels very strange. It's like being in the city and the countryside at the same time, but I really love it!

As well as being a working farm, Mudchute also has a riding school, a fantastic nature trail and a petting zoo with lots of smaller animals.

There's a restaurant where you can stop for lunch, or you can bring along a picnic to eat in the farm courtyard.

Although you can stay as long as you like, it takes about two hours to walk round and see all of the animals. If you visit the farm during the afternoon and are still there at the end of the working day, you might even get to help put some of the animals to bed!

I'd like to go here ☐

Insider tip!

The farm shop sells bags of animal food, including grass pellets and hay. I loved feeding the pigs, sharing with sheep, and letting a horse eat out of my hand! Make sure you only give them food from the shop, though. However much you like banana sandwiches or chocolate biscuits, they're really not good for animals.

All Star Bowling

All Star Lanes is one of my favourite places in London to go bowling! There are four of them in different parts of the city, and they all have a cool 1950s American diner theme. With bright colours, cute booth seats and lots of funky retro details, it feels just like the real thing.

Me and my friends love going along for giant sandwiches, hot dogs or maple-syrup pancakes before we pull on our bowling shoes, but you can also eat after you've finished your game. If I'm not super-hungry, I sometimes slurp one of their ice-cream sundaes or milkshakes instead – they're my secret bowling weapon!

You might want to book a bowling lane too, as there are a limited number in each hall, and they can get quite busy.

I'd like to go here

Look out for!

If you're bowling at Brick Lane, the hall also has private karaoke booths you can hire. They're decorated to match the vintage All Star style, and there are over 5,000 tunes for you to sing along to. You'll find a list of them online, just in case you want to sneakily practise your favourites ahead of time!

55

Cool Culture

From ballet to opera, there's no doubt London has all kinds of fabulous culture to offer. But I bet you didn't know you could watch a puppet show on a barge or that you can have a sleepover at the Science Museum or that there's even a theatre where you're not allowed to sit down! Read on to find out more. Oh, I do love my home town!

Royal Opera House and Royal Ballet

The Royal Opera House in Covent Garden is home to the Royal Opera and the Royal Ballet. It's the third theatre to stand on the same spot after two were burned down in huge fires during the 19th century.

The main theatre inside the building is shaped like a horseshoe and can seat over 2,000 people. As most operas are performed in a different language, there's a special screen above the stage where English surtitles (the opposite of subtitles!) are displayed for the audience. Some seats even have a small video screen that shows the translated words.

The Opera House also has incredible ballet performances. The Royal Ballet is the biggest ballet company in Britain, and one of the most famous in the world. Made up of around 100 dancers, they rehearse in special rooms as well as performing on stage.

Even if you don't get a chance to see a ballet or opera, you can still go on a guided tour. The brilliantly named 'Velvet, Gilt and Glamour' includes a visit to the Royal Retiring Room, where the royal family sips interval drinks when they visit!

There's also a Backstage Tour that takes you behind the scenes of what's going on in the theatre. If you're lucky you might get a glimpse of the Royal Ballet in class! If you can't decide which tour sounds best, you could always do both, like I did!

Did you know?
The Royal Opera House has its own podcast, which is free to download from the website.

I'd like to do this ☐

Museum of London

The Museum of London tells the story of the city, starting from a time when the whole population would have fitted inside just one double-decker bus! As you move through the galleries, you'll find out about the Romans, the plague, the Great Fire of London, the Victorians, the Suffragettes, the swinging Sixties and lots more. There are all kinds of displays, including some groovy vintage fashions and a super-cool retro scooter. In the main hall, you can watch a specially made London film on the museum's giant TV screens, or use the computer pods to find out more about your favourite exhibits.

Insider Tip!
Make sure you check out the museum's free phone apps before you visit. My favourite is all about the history of music in London, from what the Romans might have played at a party, right up to the coolest 21st-century tunes.

I'd like to do this ☐

Royal National Theatre

The National Theatre is on the South Bank of the River Thames, just next to Waterloo Bridge. It looks quite different to most of the older theatres in the West End, especially at night when the building is lit with fabulous coloured lights.

There are three separate theatres inside the building (my favourite is the Olivier because it's got super-glam lilac seats!), as well as places to eat and drink, hang out, listen to music or watch free performances.

How do I know so much about the place? I went on a Backstage Tour! I didn't spot any famous actors, but I did see some amazing sets being built and even got to pass round a few of the props from one show. It was so cool going to watch a play afterwards, knowing how it had all been put together. I picked up some brilliant tips for the next time me and my friends want to put on a show of our own too!

I'd like to do this

Look out for!
Watch This Space, the National Theatre's free outdoor festival happens every summer. You can go along and watch theatre, music, dancing, street performers and even circus acts outside the theatre.

Victoria and Albert Museum

The V&A (which is what most people call the museum) is the world's biggest art and design museum. With more than 100 rooms and 4.5 million objects in the museum collection, it's probably a good idea to decide what you want to look at before you start wandering round! Grab a map, and check out the collections; you can admire the precious jewels, see high fashion throughout the ages, as well as beautiful objects from countries like India, China and Japan.

Did you know?
The V&A was the first museum in the world to have a public restaurant. It's now a café, but is still the most glamorous place you'll ever scoff a sandwich!

As you walk through the museum, look out for the special 'hands-on' symbol. There are hundreds of these, and they mean you get to do all kinds of cool stuff. My favourite was trying on a fabulous Victorian costume, but you can also learn how to make theatre sound effects, build a replica of the Crystal Palace or have a go at a giant medieval slider puzzle.

I'd like to go here

Dear Daniel,

Wish you were here!

Love,
Hello Kitty
xx

Cartoon Museum

The Cartoon Museum is one of London's newest, and – in case you hadn't already guessed – it's crammed full of cartoons, comic books and caricatures. In fact, the museum library has so many books and pictures, they can't display them all at the same time! To make sure everything gets an equal chance to be shown off, they regularly change the exhibits (a bit like I do with the posters on my bedroom wall).

The displays include a mixture of things, from cartoons drawn hundreds of years ago, to brand-new comics like *The Beano* and *Doctor Who*. Some of them are really funny, while others just tell a story. Even if you don't get the jokes in some of the funny ones, they're still worth seeing because the drawings are so brilliant.

The last time I visited, I got to join in with a fun workshop on how to draw your own comic strip. The museum often has events like this, usually in the school holidays or at weekends. They run a free Family Fun Day once a month and you can sometimes meet visiting artists and cartoonists too.

I'd like to go here ☐

Look out for!
If you're a keen doodler, visit the museum website to see the winners of the Young Cartoonist of the Year competition. They're super-talented and really made me giggle!

Puppet Theatre Barge

How brilliant is the idea of watching a play on a river barge? The Puppet Theatre Barge puts on floating shows all year round, and the boat even has heating. During the summer, it sets sail for Richmond-upon-Thames, but the rest of the time the barge is moored in Little Venice, near Paddington.

The puppets used in performances are mostly marionettes – a type of puppet moved using strings or wires. They can (of course!) do all kinds of things a human actor would find impossible, which mean shows can include amazing illusions and special effects, as well as different kinds of characters and creatures.

So what kind of plays might you see on the barge? Almost anything! From traditional tales like *Aesop's Fables* to Shakespeare plays, circus-themed shows and brand-new stories written especially for the Puppet Theatre.

I'd like to go here

Insider Tip!
There are just 50 seats on board the barge, so call and reserve your tickets in advance.

Horniman Museum

The Horniman Museum is a few miles outside central London, in an area called Forest Hill. It displays objects based on natural history, musical instruments and the way people live around the world. That might sound like a funny mix of ideas, but I loved seeing things like giant African masks, a vintage drum kit and a real, stuffed walrus all in the same place!

There are lots of other stuffed animals too, plus the Nature Base and Animal Enclosure where you can see plenty of live creatures. There are even more in the museum aquarium, where I was super-smitten with the gorgeous seahorses and pretty jellyfish.

Outside the museum, you can hang out in the enormous gardens or grab a drink in the fancy glass conservatory. There's an amazing view over the rest of London and you can also follow the oldest nature trail in the city.

The museum holds lots of special art and craft workshops, as well as nature and music-themed events. There's also the Hands On Base - a whole room full of exhibits, including masks, costumes and musical instruments that you can pick up and explore as closely as you like.

I'd like to go here

Look out for!
The Centre for Understanding the Environment building. Look closely and you'll see its roof is made of real growing grass.

63

NATIONAL PORTRAIT GALLERY

National Portrait Gallery

The National Portrait Gallery is next door to the National Gallery, just off Trafalgar Square. All the portraits inside are of famous or important British people throughout history – from scientists, authors and musicians to sportspeople, movie stars and members of the royal family. Some of the portraits are painted, but you'll also spot plenty of drawings, photographs, sculptures and even video clips of famous faces.

The gallery is organised in date order, so it feels a bit like you're walking through history. You start by going up the giant escalator to the oldest paintings, and gradually work your way down to the twentieth and twenty-first centuries on the ground floor. Some of my favourite portraits are in this part of the gallery –JK Rowling, David Beckham and Darcey Bussell, the ballerina.

Those people are pretty easy to spot, but don't worry if there are loads of others you don't recognise. Head for the information desk and hire a hand-held screen with headphones that will take you on an audio

Insider Tip!
Visit the restaurant on the top floor of the gallery for an amazing view over the rooftops of London.

tour of the gallery. The touch screen has interactive maps, pictures and short films, and you can also listen to facts and stories about the people in the portraits as you walk round.

I'd like to go here ☐

London Film Museum

If you're mad about movies, make sure you don't miss a visit to the London Film Museum. It's on the first floor of the County Hall building, right next to the London Eye, and to enter the museum, you do something I've always dreamed about – walk down a red carpet!

Once you're inside, it's almost as exciting. There are original props, costumes and sets on display from films and TV shows including *Star Wars*, *Sherlock Holmes*, *Batman* and *Thunderbirds*. I especially loved the Daleks from *Doctor Who*, and Rexy from the movie, *Night At The Museum*. He moves and roars and I even got to have my picture taken with him!

Right in the middle of the museum, there's a gallery where you can find out how films are made, from the script to the glitzy opening night. Learning about behind-the-scenes stuff like sound and make-up was really cool, and you can also try making your own mini-movie trailer. There's a fun animation section, where I spotted Wallace and Gromit, and video clips showing interviews with film stars and experts.

I'd like to go here ☐

Science Museum

The Science Museum has some of the coolest, cleverest and most fun exhibits anywhere in London. With over 300,000 items to explore, there are galleries on the history of vets, flying, medicine, computers, maths, space, pattern and telephones, plus lots more!

One of my favourites is the 'Who Am I?' gallery, where you can try to work out what makes you, you. I had loads of fun working out what makes me Hello Kitty! You can do all sorts of cool experiments, like morphing your face to find out what you might look like as you get older, or hearing what you'd sound like if you were a boy. The gallery even has its own online game, *Thingdom*, on the museum website.

Another brilliant place is the Launchpad, which has over 50 interactive exhibits, as well as live shows and experiments.

Computer from the 1950s

Night at the Museum

A couple of times a month, the Science Museum holds special Science Night events, where visitors are allowed to sleep over! After an evening of exciting science-y activities, you get into your sleeping bag and nod off among the exhibits. The next morning, you wake up to a scrummy breakfast and watch a 3D IMAX movie before the museum opens for the day. You need to book ahead as it sells out super-fast.

I'd like to go here ☐

Unicorn Theatre

The Unicorn, near Tower Bridge, is London's biggest theatre for young people. As well as staging their own plays, they also host visiting productions from around the world. When I visited the super-shiny theatre, I was amazed to find out the Unicorn has actually been putting on shows for over 60 years. Then, someone told me the smart building was brand new, even if the theatre company was pretty old!

On Unicorn Family Days, you not only get to go along to the performance itself, you also take part in a fun workshop, trying out different kinds of drama, dance, art and music connected to the play. Then, after you've watched the show, it's time for tea and biscuits with the cast – you can ask them questions about the play, find out what it's like to be an actor and even get your programme signed!

I'd like to go here ☐

Insider Tip!
Tickets for most shows at the Unicorn let you pick your seats when you arrive, instead of telling you where to sit. This is a brilliant idea, but it's a good idea to get there at least half an hour before the show starts to make sure your family can get seats together.

British Museum

The British Museum is all about human history and the way people live. They have a super-huge collection of over 7 million objects, gathered from all over the world and going right back to the beginning of human history.

My top tip is to head straight for the Great Court. It's a massive space with an amazing glass roof and the museum's round reading room in the middle. There's loads of good stuff here, including the families desk where they send you out on special trails round the museum. These all have different themes, so you can pick your favourites. I tried one that was about writing, another exploring clothes, and the party-themed 'Revelling Round the World'!

You can also borrow a hand-held multimedia guide from the families desk, which helps you explore the different galleries, and also includes games and activities based on the exhibits.

As you're walking round, don't forget to look out for the Hands On desks (there are six altogether) where you can handle some of the things on display, and get an even closer look at some seriously ancient objects!

I'd like to go here ☐

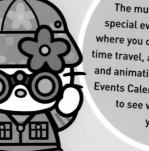

Insider tip!
The museum offers lots of special events and workshops where you can explore things like time travel, arts and crafts, history and animation. Have a look at the Events Calendar on their website to see what's on during your visit.

West End Theatres

There are over 40 theatres in London's West End. They're not all on the same street, but many of them are quite close together in an area known as Theatreland. The West End is famous for its amazing theatre shows, as well as the actors who perform in them, and millions of people visit London each year to see musicals, plays, comedies, dance and variety shows.

Look out for!
Red velvet seats, fancy gold balconies and grand chandeliers – lots of West End theatres are truly fabulous inside!

To find out what's on while you're here, you can either check the Official London Theatre website, or find listings in newspapers and magazines, including the *Evening Standard*. If you want to see a particular show, it's a good idea to book in advance, especially if you need more than two or three seats. Lots of shows sell out very quickly!

If you're not sure what you want to see, try visiting the half-price ticket booth (TKTS) – an official ticket seller, based in a funny little hut on Leicester Square. Every day, they sell tickets for some of the best West End shows at half their normal price. You have to go along in person, rather than booking over the phone, but it's a great way to see a show and save some of your holiday money too!

I'd like to go here

The Natural History Museum is home to 70 million animal, plant, rock and fossil samples, as well as one of the world's most famous dinosaurs. Dippy the Diplodocus is one of the first things you see as you walk through the entrance to the museum. He's part of a huge dinosaur collection, along with a Triceratops and a super-scary moving, roaring T-Rex!

The dinos are on display in the Blue Zone, which takes up just over a quarter of the museum, and includes plenty of other creatures too. In the other zones you can see displays on human life and the environment (Green), Earth and space (Red) and a wildlife garden (Orange).

If you want to get an even closer look at some of the exhibits (including a meteorite as old as the Earth!), check out 'Investigate', the museum's hands-on science centre. I had a brilliant time peering at things through a super-fancy microscope and trying out different kinds of scientific instruments. You can call me Genius Kitty from now on!

I'd like to go here

Scary dinosaur! Eek!

Look out for!
Keep an eye out for the 78 carved monkeys clambering across the ceiling of the museum. One is eating an apple!

Shakespeare's Globe

The first Globe Theatre was built to stage Shakespeare plays in London over 400 years ago. Shakespeare himself owned part of the theatre, until it was knocked down in 1644. The new building, Shakespeare's Globe, is very similar to the old one. The stage juts out into a circular pit, or yard, with three levels of seats around the outside. Just like the original Globe, the theatre is open air, which means it doesn't have a proper roof. The seats and stage are covered over, but if it rains, people in the pit get wet! This is all part of the atmosphere. You can buy a gallery ticket and watch the play sitting down, but I had much more fun standing in the open-air pit. You're closer to the stage and the actors, and in some plays, the action even moves off the stage and takes place right next to you! The tickets are cheaper, but make sure you wear comfy shoes because you will be standing up for a few hours – there's a strict no-sitting rule.

At the moment, the Globe only stages plays between April and October, but you can still visit all year round to go on a guided tour and explore the theatre exhibition.

> **Did you know?**
> Members of the audience who watch the show standing up in the pit are called groundlings!

I'd like to go here

Tate Modern

Tate Modern, on the south bank of the river, is a gallery of modern art from all over the world. The building looks quite different to many of London's other galleries and museums, and actually used to be a power station!

You enter the gallery through the Turbine Hall, which is an eye-popping five storeys tall. It's often used to display really big works of art that are created especially for the Tate and this huge space. To see the rest of the galleries, you then need to head upstairs. It's a good idea to grab a map at one of the information desks (you can find them on level one and level two), and then you can either find your own way round or take a multimedia tour. These tell you more about what's on display, show video clips and interviews with some of the artists and even play some cool art-related music!

There are more short films to watch in the Interactive Zone, along with fun games and activities, and you can also download the Tate Trumps mobile app to play as you walk round the rest of the gallery.

I'd like to go here

Look out for!
Keep your eyes peeled if you travel to Tate Modern by tube. The lampposts between Southwark underground station and the gallery are painted orange to show people the way.

Museum of Childhood

Insider tip!
The museum has free activities going on every single day, including tours, treasure hunts and art or craft activities.

The V&A Museum of Childhood is in east London and has the most amazing (not to mention enormous) collection of toys, games and costumes. Everything is arranged into three different galleries – Moving Toys, Creativity and Childhood – and they often have visiting exhibitions too.

In the first two galleries – Moving Toys and Creativity – I spotted rocking horses, yo-yos, superhero figures, dolls houses, old-fashioned computer games, a giant clockwork robot and, my secret favourite, a musical monkey. So cute!

The Childhood gallery is a bit different to the others. It explains how children used to live and what family life was like at different times in history. So, you can find out how children celebrated their birthdays hundreds of years ago, what they learned at school and even where they went on holiday. Did you know girls used to wear knitted woolly swimming costumes on the beach? Super-itchy!

My favourite part of the Childhood gallery was 'What We Wear', which looks at fashions over the past 300 years. There are pictures and fashion dolls as well as real clothes, and you can even try on old-fashioned shoes and hats. Don't forget to strike a vintage pose!

I'd like to go here ☐

Culture

The Illustration Cupboard

The Illustration Cupboard is an art gallery near Green Park, in central London. Although it's quite small (I promise it isn't an actual cupboard!), it's crammed full of brilliant book illustrations from artists around the world. If you enjoy reading, there's a good chance you'll recognise some of the pictures. My favourites were by Nick Sharratt (who illustrates Jacqueline Wilson's books), Lauren Child (who writes and draws *Clarice Bean* and *Ruby Redfort*) and Dick Bruna, the creator of *Miffy*.

When you've only ever seen the illustrations printed in books, it's surprising how different the original artwork looks hanging on a gallery wall. I spotted quite a few hidden details, as well as falling in love with how colourful everything looked!

I'd like to go here

Look out for!

The gallery often has special book signings, where the illustrators will autograph copies of your favourite books. Even if you can't make it to one of these, they sometimes sign extra copies, which are available to buy in the gallery.

British Music Experience

The British Music Experience at The O2 in Greenwich is an interactive museum of popular music from the last 60 years. Like most museums it has objects on display, including costumes, props and instruments belonging to some super-famous faces. But what makes it a little bit different are the interactive zones. There are eight round the outside of the exhibition, guiding you through the history of pop music, and then another six in the middle. These were my favourite part of the experience, especially the Interactive Studio, where you can get video lessons from the stars on how to play guitar, drums or keyboard! There's also a vocal booth if singing's more your thing, and a whole other zone – Dance the Decades – if you prefer dancing.

Whatever you decide to try, the studio will record your efforts, so you can watch and listen to yourself once you've finished.

I'd like to go here ☐

Insider tip!

Your British Music Experience ticket is actually a *Smarticket*! Swipe it over the sensor points as you go round, and it will save your selections or recordings. You can then log into a special online account when you get home and access everything you saved!

National Gallery

They might have very similar names, and sit next door to each other on Trafalgar Square, but the National Gallery and National Portrait Gallery are two totally separate places!

In the National Gallery, you'll find European paintings stretching from the 13th to 19th centuries, on all kinds of subjects. One of the best ways to explore them is with an audio tour, which you can hire from the Audio-Guide Desk. There are a few to choose from, including 'Teach Your Grown-ups About Art', where your parents aren't allowed to wear the headphones! The guide gives you – and only you – the lowdown on some fun arty secrets, including where you can spot mad scientists, circus performers and the grizzliest old women. It's then up to you to decide how many of the secrets you spill to the rest of your family!

Oh, and it's definitely worth popping into the gallery on a Sunday – you can join in a fun arty workshop for free.

I'd like to go here

Insider tip!

Keys to Creativity is a toolkit of ideas you can borrow from the gallery's Information Desk. It provides everything you need to start making your own drawings or even writing stories inspired by the paintings. You don't need to be a brilliant artist or writer, it's just there to help you enjoy the gallery in a different and more creative way.

Museum of Brands, Packaging and Advertising

The Museum of Brands, Packaging and Advertising is the only one of its kind anywhere in the world. It's a huge collection of posters, adverts, fashions, toys, magazines, sweets and souvenirs from the last 150 years. If you've ever wondered what your favourite brand of baked beans looked like in the 1970s, or which magazines your gran might have read when she was a little girl, this is the perfect place to find out!

The collection was started by Robert Opie when he was 16 years old. He brought home an empty sweet wrapper, but instead of throwing it away, he kept it. His collection of packaging grew, and is now so big it fills a whole museum!

The museum displays are arranged in date order, so as you walk round you can see how everyday life has changed over time. As well as simple things, like cereal packets and advertising posters, there are bigger objects, including a Chopper bike from the 1970s and the world's first portable music player, known as a Pigmy Grand.

I'd like to go here

London Transport Museum

The London Transport Museum in Covent Garden explains how people used to travel around in my home city – from trams, trains, taxis and trolleybuses to the world-famous double-decker Routemaster bus.

As you'd probably expect from a museum, there are plenty of pictures and displays to enjoy, but one of the things that's especially brilliant about the Transport Museum is that it has heaps of real buses and trains squeezed inside. It's amazing to get such a close look at buses so old they were pulled by horses instead of an engine, or to climb on board a train from the world's first underground system.

One of my favourite spots in the museum is the Interchange Gallery. As well as trying on some old-fashioned costumes there (dressing-up is always fun), I also got to sit behind the wheel of a bus driver's cab and have a go at driving a tube train. OK, so the train was only a simulator, but it felt real and I think I'd make a fabulous tube driver!

Did you know?
The huge building which is now the Transport Museum used to be part of a market selling flowers, fruit and veggies in Covent Garden!

I'd like to go here ☐

Sherlock Holmes Museum

The Sherlock Holmes Museum is at 221b Baker Street – the address Sherlock and his friend Doctor Watson shared in the famous detective stories. Whether you're a fan of Sir Arthur Conan Doyle's books, the films or the TV series, the museum is great fun to visit. My favourite part was the first-floor study, which is a brilliant, higgledy-piggledy mess of letters, pipes, pictures, bottles, books, candles and even a pistol.

Although it's based on a story, rather than real life, the study and the other rooms in the house look just as they would have done in Victorian times when the books were written. Many of the details have been taken from Sir Arthur's original descriptions, and include things like a detective's magnifying glass, police handcuffs, Sherlock's violin and some of his sneaky, but amazing, disguises.

There are some brilliant photo opportunities around the museum, so don't forget your camera. Perch one of Sherlock's deerstalker hats on your head, settle back in his fireside armchair and strike your best detective pose!

I'd like to go here

Did you know?

No one is sure exactly where the real 221b Baker Street was or if it even existed when the books were written. The museum had to get special permission to use 221b on this building, which can actually be found between number 237 and number 241 Baker Street!

Shop-a-rama

Whether you're after some super-luxury shopping in Harrods, quirky fashion boutiques like Carnaby Street or bargain hunting at London's markets, London really does have something for everyone's taste and pocket money. So, what are you waiting for? Get ready to shop till you drop!

Harrods

Harrods is probably the most famous shop in London. It's like a giant, but very posh department store, that sells clothes, jewellery, perfume, shoes, bags, make-up and fancy food. Not everything inside is as expensive as you might think, but it's fun to visit, even if you don't actually buy anything. I mostly love window-shopping, and choosing what I'd take home if I was super-rich!

I'd like to go here ☐

Insider tip!
Harrods is such a stylish store, they actually have a dress code! I always make sure I wear something cute-but-smart when I visit and carry my favourite tote bag instead of a bulky backpack.

Oxford Street

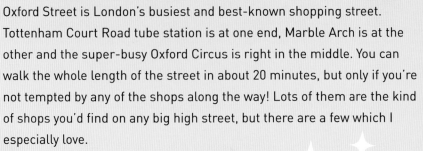

Oxford Street is London's busiest and best-known shopping street. Tottenham Court Road tube station is at one end, Marble Arch is at the other and the super-busy Oxford Circus is right in the middle. You can walk the whole length of the street in about 20 minutes, but only if you're not tempted by any of the shops along the way! Lots of them are the kind of shops you'd find on any big high street, but there are a few which I especially love.

Top Shop

Top Shop at Oxford Circus is Britain's biggest fashion store. With five floors full of clothes, shoes, accessories and make-up, it's my idea of shopping heaven. As well as racks and racks of cute outfits, the store also includes a nail bar, hair salon, vintage boutique and even has its own sweet shop. Yum!

I'd like to go here

Selfridges

Selfridges is another smart department store, with a grand entrance and lots of stuff to look at inside. They're famous for amazing displays, especially in the windows along Oxford Street. They sell just about everything, from funky stationery and posh chocolates to amazing designer outfits and the coolest gadgets around. I especially love checking out the flower shop and sneaking a sniff in the perfume department.

Super-stylish Selfridges!

I'd like to go here ☐

Did you know?
Selfridges has the biggest Beauty Hall in the world and sells 7,700 lipsticks, 2,800 mascaras and 1,000 nail polishes every week.

Playlounge

Inside, the walls are lined with quirky fluorescent honeycomb display shelves, which are super-fabulous. Each one is crammed full of weird and wonderful toys, including KidRobot figures, Miffy, Gloomy Bear goodies and adorable Ugly Dolls. Lots of the same characters also show up on other things, from T-shirts and keyrings to posters, badges and stickers.

The last time I visited the shop, I spotted an enormous Simpsons action figure that was over a metre tall. It would have been a pretty cool thing to buy, but in the end I settled on some funky wall stencils and one of my favourites, a tiny Moomin troll. As well as being quite a bit cheaper, they were much easier to carry home on the tube too!

I'd like to go here

Regent Street

Regent Street runs between Oxford Circus and Piccadilly Circus. There are plenty of shops you'll recognise, but quite a few old and unusual shops here too. I especially love Regent Street at Christmas time, when it's decorated with the most amazing lights and hanging displays.

Liberty

Even if you haven't visited or heard of Liberty before, you'll probably recognise some of their famous, flowery fabrics. You can find them in the store on all sorts of things, from scarves and bags, to watches,

Did you know?
The inside of the shop was built using wood recycled from two old ships!

sunglasses, notebooks and birthday cards. The shop itself is almost as amazing as the things it sells. On the outside, it's mostly black and white, which makes it super-easy to recognise as you're walking along the street. Once you get inside, it has a cool, creaky kind of feel, with lots of old wood panelling. My favourite bit is the lifts, which are tiny. Even if you normally take the stairs, you should definitely give the lift a try here. Just don't try to fit too many people in at once!

I'd like to go here ☐

Hamleys

Hamleys is one of the world's biggest toyshops, with over 5 million people visiting the Regent Street store every year. It's spread out over seven floors, and sells toys and games for all ages (including adults). I love watching demonstrations of the newest toys and gadgets, especially when you're allowed to try them out for

yourself! So, apart from some fabulous Hello Kitty goodies, what do they sell? Just about everything, from board games and books, to cute plushies and computer games. There's even an in-store sweet shop.

I'd like to go here ☐

Look out for!
Tantrum, the Hamleys Boutique, is a truly fabulous pampering bar. They have a team of top stylists who'll treat you like a superstar. From hair-styling to nail-painting, there are all kinds of pampering treatments you can pick from.

Camden Market

Camden Market is actually made up of six different markets, including the Stables and the Electric Ballroom. They all sort of blend together to make Camden one big amazing marketplace, especially at the weekend. Whenever I visit, I just follow the crowds and manage to find my way around really easily!

The markets are a real mish-mash of people and styles, with stalls selling all kinds of things. If you're hungry, there are also cafés and food-sellers, offering snacks from just about anywhere in the world.

My favourite bit of the markets is Camden Lock Village, near the canal. There are over 500 stalls just in this part, and lots of the stuff they sell is handmade and really unusual.

I especially like looking out for clothes, jewellery and accessories in all of the markets, although it's fun finding second-hand books and old records too. There are loads of cool retro and vintage goodies for sale, and I hardly ever leave without buying at least one funky new T-shirt for my collection!

I'd like to go here ☐

Drink, Shop & Do

Drink, Shop & Do is near King's Cross in north London. Every time I go there, I'm never sure if it's a café that also sells pretty things, or a shop with a yummy café at the back!

Both bits are decorated with super-stylish, pastel-coloured walls and retro furniture. The shop at the front sells the cutest stationery and all kinds of gorgeous crafty goodies.

In the café part, you can slurp drinks, from tasty teas and juices, to super-delicious milkshakes, floats and mocktails. They also sell cakes (including brownies – my favourite) and sandwiches.

But what makes it really unusual, is that you can buy almost everything else in the café, not just the food and drink. If your table or the chair you're sitting on has a tag, it's for sale. The pictures on the wall, the cups, the teapot and even that plant in the corner? All up for grabs! It's a really fun idea. The shop also runs arty activities. Lots of these are free, and they include card-making, playing with clay, knitting, jewellery-making and the truly fabulous dot-to-dot disco.

I'd like to go here

Look out for!
The shop has free board games that you can play at your table in the café!

Columbia Road

On a Sunday morning, Columbia Road Flower Market is probably the prettiest and best-smelling spot in London! Thousands of people head there to buy flowers, plants, fruits and veggies. The atmosphere is brilliant, but I like visiting Columbia Road for the shops, just as much as the market. There are about 60 of them altogether, selling everything

The yummy-smelling flower market!

from cupcakes to vintage clothes. Here are the ones I usually head for first.

Lapin and Me is packed with super-cute accessories and gifts. Look out for magnets, bags, badges, bracelets, notebooks and T-shirts, all decorated with adorable drawings.

Treacle is a cake shop, with the cutest name and the tastiest ever fairy cakes.

Supernice sells gorgeous gifts and pretty things for your house. The last time I visited, I bought a super-cool 'I Love London' lunchbox.

Glitterati is just as sparkly as it sounds! They sell clothes, jewellery and vintage goodies.

Suck and Chew is one of my all-time favourite sweet shops. I love their fancy chocolate butterflies and giant Love Heart sweets.

I'd like to go here ☐

Tokyo Toys

Tokyo Toys is in the London Trocadero, near to Piccadilly Circus. It's a tiny shop, packed full to bursting with Japanese toys, games and sweets. If you're a fan of anime or manga, I'm pretty sure you'll have a brilliant time browsing their busy shelves.

The things that usually catch my eye are the T-shirts, jewellery and posters, but they also sell books, trading cards, action figures, costumes and cute plushies. My absolute favourite things though, have to be the crazy-but-cool wigs in just about every style and colour you can imagine!

Insider tip!
The Trocadero isn't just a shopping centre. You can also find a cinema, games arcade, restaurants and even an underground dance area inside.

I'd like to go here ☐

Charing Cross Road

Charing Cross Road is famous for its bookshops. They sell a mixture of new and second-hand books, and quite a few of the shops specialise in a particular subject, like art, science or travel. And you might remember that the Leaky Cauldron pub in the Harry Potter series is found on Charing Cross Road! (It doesn't actually exist though!)

Foyles

Foyles is one of the oldest and best-known bookshops on Charing Cross Road. The shop is the biggest in Europe, with a mind-boggling 30 miles of bookshelves!

Inside, I love browsing for books on almost any subject, from acting to zebras, and (of course) they have plenty of brilliant stories too. Altogether, there are over 200,000 to choose from, as well as stationery, music, DVDs and magazines from around the world.

My favourite part of the shop is the children's and young adult department. Lots of the books there have been reviewed by London schoolchildren. So, if you're looking for a good read, you can check out honest opinions from someone much closer to your own age than a stuffy old adult book-reviewer!

Foyles have lots of special events, readings and book-signings, so check out the website before you plan your trip. It drives me bonkers if I visit the shop, only to discover my favourite author was autographing books there the day before!

I'd like to go here

Look out for!
It's not just books on display in the children's department at Foyles. They have a tank of bloodthirsty piranha fish too!

Qu'tse

Qu'tse is a bit further down Charing Cross Road than Foyles, and it's definitely not a bookshop. As you might have guessed from the name (it's pronounced 'cutesy'), it sells stuff that is all super-cute!

I might be a bit biased because lots of the things inside feature me, but there are lots of other lovely goodies too. My favourites are the tiny bits of stationery, from pens and pencils to tiny notepads – perfect for making lists for my next shopping trip! They also sell ornaments, jewellery, T-shirts, bags, hair accessories and lots of smaller things, like badges and magnets, which make brilliant souvenirs or presents.

Did you know?
Kawaii is Japanese for cute, pretty or lovely. It's the perfect word to describe a shop like this!

I'd like to go here

On my way to Foyles bookshop!

Paperchase

It's definitely worth going to the flagship shop on Tottenham Court Road. For a start, it's completely enormous! There are three floors, jam-packed with cute stationery, but arranged so you can easily shop for different things.

I usually start on the ground floor, which has cards, wrapping paper, postcards and the coolest present ideas and accessories. The middle floor has a café, and it's also the place you can find special products at different times of the year. I love visiting at Halloween or before Valentine's Day, but my favourite time is Christmas, when they have fabulous decorations on display.

The top floor is especially good if you like making things. As well as every kind of paint, brush, pen and pencil you can imagine, they also sell giant sheets of paper. Some of these are just plain colours, but others are handmade, or have amazing patterns and designs. The last time I visited, I found a pretty sheet covered in silver stitching, and a cool craft book that gave me some great ideas on how to use it.

Insider tip!
Check out the sale section on the third floor. It has some mega-bargains all year round.

I'd like to go here ☐

Carnaby Street

In the 1960s, Carnaby Street was the coolest place in the whole of London. With brand-new fashion boutiques and super-stylish coffee bars, it was a truly trend-setting street. Although the shops are quite different today, it's still remembered for the 'swinging sixties', when the biggest pop and film stars shopped here for their groovy gear!

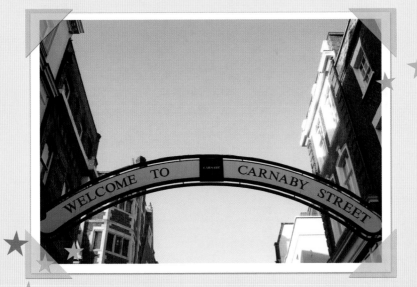

David & Goliath

David & Goliath is one of my favourite Carnaby Street shops. You shouldn't have any trouble finding it as it usually has a bubble machine right next to the entrance. They sell really cute underwear and pyjama sets, but the things they do best are T-shirts. Most of them include silly slogans or cartoons, and each range has its own fun name, like 'Trendy Wendy' or 'Boys Are Smelly'! The tees themselves are plain and simple styles in lots of different colours, and there's bound to be at least one that makes you grin.

I'd like to go here

Searching for a bargain!

Petticoat Lane

Petticoat Lane Market is London's famous Sunday street market. Amazing as it sounds, there's been a market here in the same spot for over 250 years. It was named after the petticoats and fancy lace that were once sold in the area, but you're now much more likely to find bargain clothes, jewellery, shoes, toys and gadgets here. With over 1,000 stalls, the market spreads out into 10 different streets and is open from 9am to 2pm.

Don't get confused looking for a street sign that says 'Petticoat Lane' – it doesn't exist. Today, the market happens in and around Middlesex Street. The Victorians renamed Petticoat Lane because they didn't like the idea of a street named after a type of ladies' underwear! It didn't really work, though – even now, most people still call it Petticoat Lane.

I'd like to go here

Angels Fancy Dress

Angels Fancy Dress has been hiring out costumes to actors since 1840. They now sell them to the public as well, from a fabulous 6-floor shop on Shaftesbury Avenue.

I love going along to visit them if I'm off to a fancy-dress party. They have just about every kind of costume you can imagine, from superheroes and pop stars, to characters from your favourite cartoons and movies. None of these were quite what I was looking for the last time I went to the shop, so the staff helped me pick out something different. I went to my party dressed as a Crayola crayon, in a costume that was silly and fun, but still kind of super-stylish too!

Even if you're not looking for a costume, there are still lots of fun accessories to browse. Their fabulous fake jewellery and tiaras make perfect over-the-top party accessories, and they have fun bags, shoes and hats too. For general silliness (or April Fools!), I also love checking out the false noses, fake teeth and silly wigs!

I'd like to go here

Look out for!
The shop has dressed up some super-famous faces, and lots of them have left special messages in the visitors book. You can find some of them online at the Angels website.

Covent Garden

I love hanging out in Covent Garden! It's one of my favourite London spots, especially in summer. I can shop, go to the theatre, eat in all different kinds of cafés or just sit and watch some of the amazing street performers. The ones I like best are the jugglers and mime artists, and there's usually a band or busker you can listen to as well. Right in the middle of Covent Garden's busy streets is the Piazza. It's a giant square with shops and cafés round the outside. Something is always going on there, even if it's raining!

One of my favourite markets!

The Apple Market

Covent Garden used to be a huge fruit and vegetable market. You're much more likely to find cupcakes and cute clothes there now, but the Apple Market is still named after a little piece of its fruity history.

There are actually a few different markets in Covent Garden, but the Apple is the one I visit most often. It's in the Piazza and has about forty stalls. They mostly sell arts and crafts, or handmade goods, so it's the perfect place to pick up an unusual bracelet or one-of-a-kind hat. As well as jewellery and accessories, they also sell clothes, gifts and sometimes toys. One of the cool things about the market is that the stalls change all the time, so you never know what you might find on your next visit.

I'd like to go here

Did you know?
Piazza is the Italian word for a paved city square.

Magma

There are two Magma shops in Covent Garden, and they're quite close together. One of them sells books, but it's the other shop I really love to visit. It's like a stationery shop, an art shop and a cool toy shop, all rolled into one. They sell cards, posters, gadgets, jewellery and there's also a fun 'weird stuff' section. I love their reels of fancy sticky-tape, although my favourite thing has to be the amazing kits that let you build a real, working camera from cardboard!

I'd like to go here

Shop

Tatty Devine

Tatty Devine is the coolest jewellery shop in town. They sell fun and funky accessories in bright colours and super-trendy designs. From necklaces and bracelets, to rings and brooches, they have all the types of jewellery you'd expect, but in very different shapes. I spotted squirrels, puppies, shoes, moustaches, bananas and some googly, cartoon eyes!

Lots of famous faces wear Tatty jewellery, and it often appears in big fashion magazines too. Although some of the things in the shop are quite expensive, there are also plenty of cheaper things. My favourite-ever find was a ring with whiskers and cat ears – totally fabulous!

I'd like to go here

Seven Dials

Seven Dials is just on the edge of Covent Garden. It's made up of seven streets, which all meet or cross over at the same spot. There are some really cool shops in the area, and I love the fact that it feels like a more secret, hidden part of Covent Garden than the busy Piazza.

Bead Heaven

The London Bead Shop is like a tiny treasure chest, bursting with bead-y goodness. Some of them cost just a few pence, and there are hundreds to choose from. I spotted beads in just about every size and shape, along with charms, gems and crystals in a rainbow of colours. My favourite find was a tray of little pig-shaped beads – so cute! You don't need to know anything in particular about beads to enjoy shopping here. It's like a DIY jewellery shop, and is totally perfect for beginners. If you can thread beads on to a piece of string or elastic, you can make your own jewellery. They even sell the thread and elastic to get you started!

Bead Aura sells beads and findings (the bits you need to turn beads into things like earrings or hair-clips), along with jewellery kits, and books and magazines about jewellery-making. You can also buy ready-made bead necklaces and bracelets if you're feeling lazy.

Beadworks is the biggest and oldest bead shop in Covent Garden. They sell beautiful beads from around the world, made out of wood, glass, plastic, metal, shell, pearls and even china! Keep an eye out for the sparkliest sequins, and beads you can sew to your clothes too. If you're not sure what you'd like to make, take a closer look at the walls round the shop. They're filled with gorgeous pieces of jewellery made by the shop staff, and displayed to give you lots of ideas and inspiration.

I'd like to go here ☐

King's Road

King's Road in west London stretches between Sloane Square and an area known as World's End in Chelsea. It was especially famous for its super-stylish fashion boutiques during the 1960s and 1970s. It's still one of the most fashionable parts of the city, and you can find lots of fabulous shops along the road.

Artbox

Artbox is my idea of shopping heaven. It sells funky Korean and Japanese goodies, including lots of Hello Kitty (hello!).

Picking out my favourites is super-tricky, because everything is so cute. They sell papery stuff – including letter sets, stickers, cards and an origami dress-up doll, which I love. And then there are accessories, like make-up bags, headphones, hair bobbles and shoes with panda faces.

I'd like to go here ☐

Insider tip!
Check out the 'home' section: there are even fun bandages and plasters, so your cuts and scrapes can look as stylish as the rest of your outfit!

9

VV Rouleaux

VV Rouleaux, near Sloane Square, sells ribbon and fancy trimmings. The shop isn't huge, but it is amazing. Packed with ruffles, lace, tassels, feathers, beads, bobbles, pom-poms, sequins and ribbon in just about every colour and style you can think of, it's gorgeous enough to make me dizzy!

If you're crafty and creative, you'll love it, but you really don't need any special skills to use the things they sell. I love picking out pieces of polka-dot ribbon, velvet trim or sparkly sequinned shapes, and then using them to revamp my old clothes. Plus ribbon looks lovely wrapped round a parcel.

I'd like to go here

Portobello Road

Portobello Market in Notting Hill takes up nearly all of Portobello Road – a long, narrow street that is about two miles long. It's filled with hundreds of stalls, and there are also cafés, restaurants and shops along the way. Portobello is just as popular with locals and people from other parts of London as it is with tourists. They visit to shop for antiques, food, fashion, jewellery and brilliant bargains!

I always get off the tube at Notting Hill Gate, and walk down Portobello Road. If you do the same, the first bit of the market you'll come to is antiques. Next, it's

food – mostly fruit, veggies, bread, cheese and tasty cakes. After that, you'll find stalls selling new-but-cheap things (mostly boring stuff, like batteries and socks), and then comes my favourite – fashion! You can find some super-amazing outfits, and you might even get the chance to spot a few designers before they become famous and successful.

I'd like to go here

Look out for!
The market is open six days a week, but it's not the same every day. I especially love the Saturday market because it includes craft stalls that sell cute handmade jewellery and accessories.

Shop

The Royal Borough of Kensington and Chelsea
PORTOBELLO ROAD, W.11

Fashion, fruit and fun!

Eats and Treats

One thing's for sure, you're spoilt for choice when it comes to fabulous places to eat in London. Whatever you're in the mood for, you'll always find something to tickle your fancy whether you're looking for a quick snack, a big meal or a seriously scrummy ice cream.

Here are some of my favourite places for you. (There are so many of them that I've divided them up into super-easy-to-follow sections for you!) Happy eating!

Eat

Oh, and if you're looking for a yummy restaurant in a particular area, simply check out my easy-to-follow colour-coded cards.

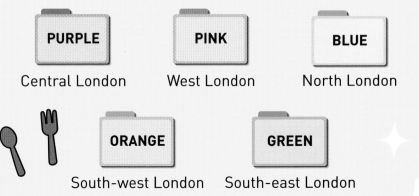

PURPLE
Central London

PINK
West London

BLUE
North London

ORANGE
South-west London

GREEN
South-east London

Serious Scoffing

My Old Dutch

131–132 High Holborn, WC1V 6PS

www.myolddutch.com

☎ 020 7242 5200

⊖ Holborn

Did you know?
The first My Old Dutch restaurant opened in London over 50 years ago!

Ingredients

- Delicious fresh pancakes with sweet and savoury fillings.
- Traditional Dutch starters and puddings, including warm waffles with the tastiest toppings.
- A fun and friendly atmosphere, perfect for family visits.

Giraffe

11 Frith Street, W1D 4RB

www.giraffe.net

☎ 020 7494 3491

⊖ Leicester Square

Look out for!
There are over 15 Giraffe restaurants in London. Check the website to find them all.

Ingredients

- Tasty breakfast and brunch food, as well as snacks and meals to enjoy later in the day.
- Hot chocolate and fresh fruit smoothies.
- Food inspired by cooking and recipes from around the world.

Rainforest Café

20 Shaftesbury Avenue, W1D 7EU

www.therainforestcafe.co.uk

☎ 020 7434 3111

⊖ Piccadilly Circus

Look out for!
The stools have animal legs and tails. They look really funny when people are sitting on them!

Ingredients

- Amazing fake-rainforest decoration with giant trees, vines, toadstools, a waterfall and a real aquarium.
- Jungle sound effects and a fun gift shop.
- Lots of different types of food to choose from, including burgers, pasta, noodles and fish.

Ed's Easy Diner

12 Moor Street, W1D 5NG

www.edseasydiner.co.uk

☎ 020 7434 4439

⊖ Leicester Square

Ingredients

- Funky, 1950s-style theme and decoration.
- American-style hamburgers, hot dogs, fries and shakes (including my favourite peanut-butter flavour. Yum!).
- Super-cool vintage jukeboxes, where you can chose which record you want to play.

Eat

Leon

73-76 Strand, WC2R 0DE

www.leonrestaurants.co.uk

☎ 020 7240 3070

⊖ Charing Cross

Insider tip!
Not near the Strand? There are eight more Leons all over London!

Ingredients

- Fast food and snacks that are healthy, natural and tasty.
- Sandwiches, salads, meatballs and curry, plus fresh juice, delicious cakes and the best brownies ever!
- Kind to the planet, with recycled furniture and eco-friendly packaging.

Sticky Fingers

Did you know?
Sticky Fingers is owned by a member of super-famous 1960s rock band, *The Rolling Stones*.

1 Phillimore Gardens, W8 7QB

www.stickyfingers.co.uk

☎ 020 7938 5338

⊖ High Street Kensington

Ingredients

- American-style food, with burgers, giant sandwiches and brilliant barbecue ribs.
- Old guitars and cool music posters all over the walls.
- Ice-cream floats and lots of sweet treats, including the delicious Sticky Sundae!

The Honest Sausage

The Broad Walk, Regent's Park, NW1 4NU

www.companyofcooks.com

☎ 020 7224 3872

⊖ Baker Street

Look out for!
There's another Honest Sausage in Greenwich Park!

Ingredients

- Right in the middle of Regent's Park, with wooden benches and tables so you can sit outside.
- Juicy, mouth-watering sausages in soft bread rolls.
- Homemade cakes and puddings.

Maxwell's Bar & Grill

8 James Street, Covent Garden, WC2E 8BH

www.maxwells.co.uk

☎ 020 7395 5804

⊖ Covent Garden

Insider tip!
Lots of people visit Maxwell's as a handy place to have a meal before they go to the theatre.

Ingredients

- Big, exciting and right in the middle of Covent Garden.
- Tasty grilled foods including chicken, burgers, nachos, fresh fish and veggie meals too.
- Famous banana-split puddings, and lip-licking malted milkshakes!

Eat

107

N-ice and Sweet

Scoop

40 Short's Gardens, WC2H 9AB

www.scoopgelato.com

☎ 020 7240 7086

⊖ Covent Garden

Insider tip!
If the shop isn't too busy, the friendly staff will usually give you a little sample to taste so you can decide which flavour to order!

Ingredients

- Delicious Italian gelato (ice cream) and fresh, fruity sorbets.
- A tasty rainbow of ice-cream flavours (the nutty ones are my favourites!)
- Scrummy waffles and pancakes, plus big, waffley cones for your gelato.

Snog

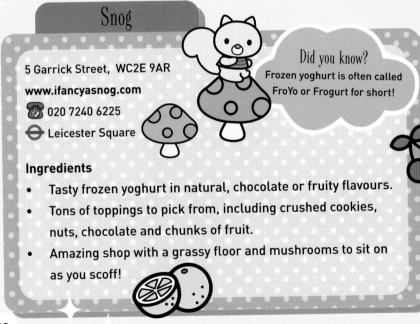

5 Garrick Street, WC2E 9AR

www.ifancyasnog.com

☎ 020 7240 6225

⊖ Leicester Square

Did you know?
Frozen yoghurt is often called FroYo or Frogurt for short!

Ingredients

- Tasty frozen yoghurt in natural, chocolate or fruity flavours.
- Tons of toppings to pick from, including crushed cookies, nuts, chocolate and chunks of fruit.
- Amazing shop with a grassy floor and mushrooms to sit on as you scoff!

Oddono's

14 Bute Street, SW7 3EX

www.oddonos.com

☎ 020 7052 0732

⊖ South Kensington

Did you know?
Since they opened in 2004, Oddono's have made ice cream in over 130 different flavours!

Ingredients

- Ice cream and sorbet made with tasty natural ingredients.
- Flavours include favourites like strawberry and chocolate, plus more unusual things like pistachio, coconut and mango.
- Show-kitchen in the shop, so you can watch as the ice cream is made.

Cybercandy

3 Garrick Street, WC2E 9BF

www.cybercandy.co.uk

☎ 08458 380958

⊖ Leicester Square

Insider tip!
I've heard a rumour Cybercandy sell Hello Kitty lollies, chocolate bars and jellybeans!

Ingredients

- Two floors full of tasty sweets from all over the world.
- Weird as well as wonderful sweets, including salty liquorice, sushi lollipops and cheese-flavoured chocolate bars!
- Rare and limited editions, plus hard-to-find soft drinks and breakfast cereals.

Eat

109

Lick Gelato

55 Greek Street, W1D 3DT

www.lick-gelato.com

☎ 020 8617 0042

⊖ Tottenham Court Road

Did you know?
Gelato is very similar to ice cream, but not exactly the same. Give it a try and see if you can taste the difference!

Ingredients

- Funky, friendly and full of home-made Italian ice cream.
- Weird and wonderful flavours, like watermelon, sesame seed, Nutella, honey puff and apple pie.
- Next to Soho Square, so on a sunny day you can sit on the grass and scoff outdoors!

Hope and Greenwood

1 Russell Street, WC2B 5JD

www.hopeandgreenwood.co.uk

☎ 020 7240 3314

⊖ Covent Garden

Insider tip!
Hope and Greenwood love inventing new sweets such as Sugar Plums and Gingerbread Humbugs!

Ingredients

- Shelves filled to the ceiling with multi-coloured sweets.
- Super-cool old-fashioned treats, including toffee, chocolate, bonbons, marshmallows and jellies.
- The cutest red and white stripy paper bags for carrying your sweets home!

MADD

53 Rupert Street, W1D 7PH

www.wearemadd.com

☎ 020 7434 3588

⊖ Piccadilly Circus

Insider tip!
It might sound super-obvious, but if you don't like mangoes, this isn't the place for you!

Ingredients

- Crazy café where almost everything on the menu includes mango!
- Smoothies and puddings, including mango mousse, mango pancakes and mango cupcakes, but also savoury mango rice.
- Bright and funky inside, with games like Jenga and Connect Four to play at your table.

Eat

Going Green

Tibits

12–14 Heddon Street, W1B 4DA

www.tibits.co.uk

☎ 020 7758 4110

⊖ Tottenham Court Road

Insider tip!
When you weigh your plate of food, take off any bread first – it comes free with the rest of your meal!

Ingredients

- Healthy-but-delicious vegetarian food that you can pick and mix however you like.
- Fill your plate from the super-cool 'food boat', then weigh it to work out the price!
- Stylish and bright inside, with cosy sofas downstairs and blackboard walls you can draw on!

Mildred's Vegetarian

45 Lexington Street

www.Mildreds.co.uk

☎ 020 7494 1634

⊖ Piccadilly Circus

Ingredients

- Funky, friendly and full of home-made Italian ice cream.
- Weird and wonderful flavours, like watermelon, sesame seed, Nutella, honey puff and apple pie.
- Next to Soho Square, so on a sunny day you can sit on the grass and scoff outdoors!

Beatroot

92 Berwick Street, W1F 0QD

www.beatroot.org.uk

☎ 020 7437 8591

🚇 Piccadilly Circus

Ingredients

- Cool café serving healthy and delicious vegetarian food.
- Scrummy selection of vegan cakes and smoothies made using fresh fruit from the market outside!
- All sorts of salads, plus (veggie) sausage rolls, stir-fry, rice, pasta and soup.

Greens and Beans

131 Drummond Street, NW1 2HL

www.greensandbeans.co.uk

☎ 020 7380 0857

🚇 Euston

Insider tip!
Takeaway lunches are packed into small, medium or large containers. You pay for the size you want, then cram as much food inside as you can!

Ingredients

- Veggie meals and snacks to take away or eat in the super-stylish basement café.
- The best veggie pizzas and soup so good it sells out most days!
- Cool breakfasts and a different lunch menu for each day of the week.

Eat

Slurp

Bubbleology

49 Rupert Street, W1D 7PF

www.bubbleology.co.uk

☎ 0207 494 4231

🚇 Piccadilly Circus

Insider tip!
Bubble tea is delicious! It can be served hot or cold, and has balls of natural, chewy tapioca at the bottom.

Ingredients

- Flavoured fruit or milk tea, ready to mix and match with your favourite bubble flavours.
- Choose from chewy, jelly-like bubbles or exploding pearls that pop in your mouth.
- Shop decorated to look like the world's cutest chemistry set, with staff dressed in white lab coats!

Crussh

14 Broadwick Street, W1F 8HP

www.crussh.com

☎ 020 7287 4480

🚇 Oxford Circus

Insider tip!
Most drinks are made while you wait, so you can swap ingredients round or leave out the ones you don't like to make the perfect, slurp-able treat!

Ingredients

- Smart and super-stylish juice bar, with more than 20 branches all over London.
- Made-to-order fruit juice pressed on the spot and thick, scrummy smoothies whizzed up as you watch!
- Sandwiches, salads, sushi, soup and other snacks to eat in or take away.

Shake It!

26 Greenwich Church Street, SE10 9BJ

www.shakeitgreenwich.co.uk

☎ 020 8853 2364

⊖ Cutty Sark [DLR]

Look out for!
I haven't dared to try one yet, but they also sell Marmite milkshakes!

Ingredients

- Milkshake shop, with over 100 different flavours, plus juice and smoothies.
- Super-tasty shakes made by mixing milk and ice cream with your favourite sweets or chocolate bars.
- Most flavours are also available as hot milkshakes if you're feeling chilly.

Eat

Jet-Setting

Los Locos

24-26 Russell Street, WC2B 5HF

www.los-locos.co.uk

☎ 020 7379 0220

⊖ Covent Garden

Ingredients

- Fun, buzzy restaurant, serving Mexican and Tex-Mex food.
- Nachos, enchiladas, refried beans and fajitas, plus tasty burgers and lots of things to share.
- Mocktails to drink, including my favourite – a Salty Puppy!

Wahaca

80 Wardour Street, W1F 0TF

www.wahaca.co.uk

☎ 020 7734 0195

⊖ Piccadilly Circus

Insider tip!
Most Wahaca waiters are happy to help you out if you're not sure what to order – just ask for their advice.

Ingredients

- Stylish restaurant inspired by the food sold in Mexican street markets.
- Tacos, tortillas and burritos, plus 'small plates' for sharing or trying a little taste of everything.
- Lip-smacking drinks, including ginger beer, soda and traditional Mexican flower juice!

Imli

167-168 Wardour Street, W1F 8WR

www.imli.co.uk

☎ 020 7287 4243

⊖ Piccadilly Circus

Insider Tip!
Imli serve dishes 'tapas-style' – so it's super-perfect for sharing with your family or friends.

Ingredients

- Indian food that's deliciously spicy, but not too hot.
- Small dishes (including plenty for vegetarians), so you can mix and match to make your perfect meal.
- Colourful, chilled-out and super-friendly!

Masala Zone

48 Floral Street, WC2E 9DA

www.masalazone.com

☎ 020 7379 0101

⊖ Covent Garden

Insider tip!
Masala Zone is next door to the grand (and huge) Royal Opera House, so you shouldn't have any trouble finding your way there!

Ingredients

- Tasty and traditional Indian street food, including curry, grills, crunchy salads and different side dishes every day.
- Drinks including pomegranate or watermelon juice, plus cool lassis, made from frothy, whipped yoghurt.
- Amazing decorations inside, including fish-eye mirrors and hundreds of colourful Indian puppets hanging from the ceiling!

Eat

Gourmet Pizza

Gabriel's Wharf, Upper Ground, SE1 9PP

☎ 020 7928 3188

Ⓣ Waterloo

Look out for!
The outdoor area has a heater, so you can still sit outside, even on chilly evenings!

Ingredients

- Right next to the river, with amazing views on sunny days and at night.
- Busy, buzzy area with cool shops and lots to do nearby.
- Tons of tasty pizzas with a mixture of old favourites and unusual new toppings.

Vapiano

19-21 Great Portland Street, W1W 8QB

www.vapiano.co.uk

☎ 020 7268 0082

Ⓣ Oxford Circus

Insider tip!
You won't be bored if you have to wait for a table. The kitchen has glass walls, so you can watch the chefs making (and throwing) the pizza dough!

Ingredients

- Yummy pizza and pasta meals, with lots of big salads too.
- Special garden area in the middle of the restaurant, where all the herbs and salads are grown.
- Super-whizzy chip card system for ordering your food.

Ping Pong Dim Sum

29a James Street, W1U 1DZ

www.pingpongdimsum.co.uk

☎ 020 7034 3100

⊖ Bond Street

Insider tip!
Check the website to find Ping Pongs in other parts of London.

Ingredients

- Sleek and super-stylish Chinese restaurant, or teahouse.
- Dim sum (bite-sized snacks), including prawn crackers, spicy seaweed, spring rolls and dumplings.
- The prettiest and most delicious drinks, including mocktails and flowering tea!

Wagamama

Insider tip!
Each bit of your order is delivered as soon as it's ready. Tuck in straight away – if you wait for the rest to arrive, it might go cold!

Riverside Level, Royal Festival Hall, SE1 8XX

www.wagamama.com

☎ 020 7021 0877

⊖ Waterloo

Ingredients

- Japanese noodle bar, with tables outside overlooking the river.
- Traditional ramen noodles, plus sticky rice, satay, soup, salad and (my favourite) coloured pickles.
- Cool electronic system that zaps your order straight to the kitchen, so they can get cooking!

Eat

119

Cha Cha Moon

15-21 Ganton Street, W1F 9BN

www.chachamoon.com

☎ 020 7297 9800

⊖ Oxford Circus

Ingredients

- Super-fast Asian food, with open kitchens so you can watch the chefs as they cook!
- Chinese curry, fishcakes, crispy salads and noodles with chicken, beef or fish.
- Delicious fruit fritters for pudding, plus mocktails and fancy juices to drink.

Nécco

52-54 Exmouth Market, EC1R 4QE

www.necco.co.uk

☎ 020 7713 8575

⊖ Farringdon

Did you know?
Nécco is the Japanese word for cat.

Ingredients

- Pretty, pink and super-cute inside!
- Delicious Japanese food, from sushi and rice bowls to dumplings and fancy cakes.
- Tasty takeaways at lunchtime in a traditional Bento box.

Kulu Kulu

76 Brewer Street, W1F 9TU

www.kulukulu.co.uk

☎ 020 7734 7316

⊖ Piccadilly Circus

Insider tip!
The best thing about picking sushi from a conveyor belt is that you don't have to know how to pronounce what you want. If it looks tasty, just help yourself!

Ingredients

- Japanese sushi restaurant with food delivered on a fun conveyor belt, and cooked in the middle by a chef as you watch.

- A mixture of raw and cooked food, including scrummy sushi made with fish, rice, veggies and crispy seaweed.

- As much free tea as you can drink!

Eat

121

Hey, Cupcake!

Candy Cakes

Covent Garden Piazza, WC2E 8RA

www.candycakes.com

☏ 020 7836 9982

Ⓣ Covent Garden

Insider tip!
The cupcakes are huge, which makes them perfect for sharing!

Ingredients

- Cute and colourful cake shop, with the prettiest counter and window display, plus seats so you can eat outdoors.
- Fabulous flavours including banana, toffee, raspberry-apple, red velvet and American cheesecake.
- Crazy-coloured frosting made with natural ingredients, and topped with fun sweeties.

The Parlour, Fortnum and Mason

181 Piccadilly, W1A 1ER

www. fortnumandmason.com

☏ 020 7734 8040

Ⓣ Piccadilly Circus

Look out for!
With a choice between smoothies, milkshakes, floats and super-creamy hot chocolate, deciding what you want to drink is hard work!

Ingredients

- Chic, retro-style café on the top floor of posh department store, Fortnum and Mason.
- Afternoon tea, with scones and jam, tasty cakes and sandwiches.
- Amazing ice creams and sundaes, including banana splits and a mouth-watering knickerbocker glory!

Bea's of Bloomsbury

44 Theobalds Road, WC1X 8NW

www. beasofbloomsbury.com

☎ 020 7242 8330

⊖ Chancery Lane

Look out for!
Just when you thought cakes couldn't get any better, I spotted one here with edible glitter sprinkled on top. Wow!

Ingredients

- Breakfast muffins, pastries, sandwiches and, in the summer, picnic hampers packed and ready to take away!
- Pretty cupcakes, squidgy brownies and colourful macaroons.
- Bakery and cake shop, with a smart-but-pretty café that's perfect for afternoon tea.

Primrose Bakery

42 Tavistock Street, WC2E 7PB

www.primrosebakery.org.uk

☎ 020 7836 3638

⊖ Covent Garden

Ingredients

- Super-pretty pastel-coloured cupcake bakery with chairs and tables.
- Delicious flavours, including rose, violet, coconut, peanut butter and vanilla with sprinkles.
- Cupcakes in two sizes – regular and tiny, which are perfect if you want to try more than one flavour!

Eat

123

Sweet Couture Cake Boutique

23b New Row, Covent Garden, WC2N 4LA

www.sweetcouture.co.uk

☎ 020 7836 8231

Ⓣ Leicester Square

Insider tip!
Make sure you don't miss it as you walk past – the shop does actually look like a boutique instead of a bakery from the outside!

Ingredients

- Small but super-fashionable cake shop.
- Freshly-baked cupcakes, topped with cream cheese or buttercream frosting and super-stylish decorations.
- Slices of home-made cake, muffins and brownies, and yummy hot chocolate to wash them down!

Hummingbird Bakery

155a Wardour Street, W1F 8WG

www.hummingbirdbakery.com

☎ 020 7851 1795

Ⓣ Tottenham Court Road

Did you know?
The Hummingbird Bakery has its own cook book if you want to try making your favourite cakes when you get home!

Ingredients

- Super-delicious cakes, cupcakes, pies, brownies and whoopie pies.
- Special 'cupcake of the day' flavours, including black bottom, popcorn, carrot-cake and strawberry milkshake.
- Gorgeously girly pink and chocolate-coloured shop, with super-cute cupcake pics on the walls!

My Favourite London food

⭐ My favourite place that I ate in London was ....

⭐ I went there on .... with ....

⭐ I ate .... It was super-yummy.

⭐ I drank .... It was lip-smackingly good.

⭐ I wish I'd had room for ....

⭐ Next time, I'm definitely going to order ....

⭐ I would give it .... out of 10.

Draw or stick a picture of yourself tucking into your favourite London food here! Mmm, yummy!

Eat

Travel and Transport

Want to know the best way to travel when you're in London? Check out my super-smart guide to the different types of transport, and you'll be whizzing round like a local in no time at all!

Buses

London's famous red buses are easy to spot on the streets, but they can seem complicated at first. There are so many, heading in all directions and stopping off all over the place! Instead of reading the timetables at a bus stop, I just look at the names on the front of the bus itself. There might be eight or nine altogether, but if 'South Kensington' is one of them, I know it'll drop me off somewhere near my favourite museum. If you miss your stop on the bus, don't panic! They're usually pretty close together, so you can just get off at the next one and walk back.

Good about buses

You get some amazing views of the city on a bus. Sit on the top deck of a double-decker, and you'll see things from up there that you'd never spot on foot or in a cab.

Not so good about buses

The traffic jams in London are almost as famous as the buses. If you get stuck in one, it can make your journey slow, boring and (in the end) super-annoying!

Underground

The London Underground is the oldest in the world. Most people call it the tube (because that's what shape the tunnels are!), and it's one of the fastest ways to travel around the city. Each line on the underground is colour-coded, which makes it easier to find your way around. You can pick up a free tube map in most stations, and it's easy to spot stations, thanks to the red and blue underground signs outside.

Good about tubes

You don't have to worry about the traffic, because you're whizzing along underneath it! At the busiest stations, trains arrive every few minutes, so you never have to wait too long.

Not so good about tubes

They can get hot, stuffy and very overcrowded, especially in summer. I try not to travel early in the morning or at the end of the afternoon when the tube is crammed with people going to and from work.

Did you know?

The tube is one of the busiest travel systems in the world. It carries over four million passengers per day!!

Trains

Normal trains are often called overground trains in London. They leave from stations including Victoria, Waterloo, Paddington, Euston and Liverpool Street. They travel to lots of places in outer London where there are no tubes, and also to other parts of the UK.

Transport

127

DLR

The Docklands Light Railway (or DLR) is very similar to the tube, and some of the trains run out of underground stations. It's useful for reaching places in east and south London where there are no underground stations.

Taxis

Black cabs can be useful, especially if you're in a hurry or when it's raining. Cab drivers are often really interesting, and have some amazing stories about London. A cab is just as likely to get stuck in traffic as a bus, but the drivers know lots of sneaky shortcuts that buses can't take!

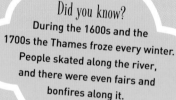

Boats

Did you know?
During the 1600s and the 1700s the Thames froze every winter. People skated along the river, and there were even fairs and bonfires along it.

Depending on where you're travelling to and from, you might be able to go by boat or river-taxi. I don't get a chance to use it very often, but it's definitely my favourite kind of London transport – it's like going on a mini sightseeing trip! Thames Clipper boats leave every 20–30 minutes from over 10 different piers along the river. They're much fancier than tubes and buses, with snacks, drinks and even plasma-screen TVs on board.

Travelcards and Oyster

Buying a ticket each time you travel on a bus, tube or train can get very expensive. It's much cheaper to bag yourself an Oyster or travelcard, which lets you make as many journeys as you like for a set price.

Travelcards are paper tickets. You can buy a one-day or seven-day travelcard from underground or train stations, and start using it straight away. A one-day card is more expensive if you want to travel before 9.30 in the morning.

Oyster cards are electronic tickets. They're made from plastic and you swipe them over a special card-reader at the start and end of your journey.

Insider tip!
If you're under 16, you can travel for free on some kinds of London transport. Visit the TfL website, or ask at a station when you arrive to find out more.

My favourite way to travel around London is:

On the tube ☐

On the train ☐

On the bus ☐

On foot ☐

On a bike ☐

By taxi ☐

By boat ☐

Hello Kitty's Address Book

Angels Fancy Dress
119 Shaftesbury Avenue, WC2H 8AE
☎ 020 7836 5678
www.fancydress.com
⦿ Leicester Square

All Star Lanes (Brick Lane)
95 Brick Lane, E1 6QL
☎ 020 7426 9200
www.allstarlanes.co.uk
⦿ Aldgate East

All Star Lanes (Holborn)
Victoria House, Bloomsbury Place,
WC1B 4DA
☎ 020 7025 2676
www.allstarlanes.co.uk
⦿ Holborn

Artbox
Kings Walk Centre
122 Kings Road, SW3 4TR
☎ 020 7581 3422
www.artbox.co.uk
⦿ Sloane Square

BBC Tour
BBC Television Centre
Wood Lane, W12 7RJ
☎ 0370 901 1227
www.bbc.co.uk/showsandtours
⦿ White City or Wood Lane

Bead Aura
3 Neal's Yard, WC2H 9DP
☎ 020 7836 3002
www.beadaura.co.uk
⦿ Covent Garden or Leicester Square

Beadworks (The Bead Shop)
21a Tower Street, WC2H 9NS
☎ 020 7240 0931
www.beadworks.co.uk
⦿ Covent Garden or Leicester Square

BFI IMAX Cinema
1 Charlie Chaplin Walk, SE1 8XR
☎ 020 7199 6000
www.bfi.org.uk/bfi_imax
⦿ Waterloo

Big Ben and the Houses of Parliament
St Margaret Street, SW1A 0AA
☎ 0844 847 1672
www.parliament.uk/visiting
⦿ Westminster

British Museum
Great Russell Street, WC1B 3DG
☎ 020 7323 8299
www.britishmuseum.org
⦿ Russell Square or Holborn

British Music Experience
The O2, Greenwich Peninsula, SE10 0DX
☎ 020 8463 2000
www.britishmusicexperience.com
⦿ North Greenwich

Brit Movie Tours
☎ 0844 247 1007
Britmovietours.com

Brockwell Lido
Brockwell Park, Dulwich Road,
SE24 0PA
☎ 020 7274 3088
🚇 Herne Hill (overground)

Buckingham Palace
SW1A 1AA
☎ 020 7766 7300
www.royalcollection.org.uk
🚇 Victoria or St James' Park

Camden Market
Camden High Street/Chalk Farm Road, NW1
www.camden-market.org
🚇 Camden Town

Captain Kidd's Canary
Wharf Voyage Boarding Gate One, London
Eye Millennium Pier, London, SE1 7PB
☎ 0207 928 8933
www.londonribvoyages.com
🚇 Waterloo

The Cartoon Museum
35 Little Russell Street, WC1A 2HH
☎ 020 7580 8155
www.cartoonmuseum.org
🚇 Russell Square or Holborn

Columbia Road Market
Columbia Road, E2
www.columbiaroad.info
🚇 Old Street

Covent Garden
Covent Garden Piazza/Apple Market,
WC2E 8RD
www.coventgardenlondonuk.com
🚇 Covent Garden

Crystal Palace Park
Thicket Road, SE20 8DT
☎ 020 8778 9496
🚇 Crystal Palace or Penge West

David & Goliath
15 Carnaby Street, W1F 9PN
☎ 020 7434 9804
www.chicksrule.co.uk/carnaby-street
🚇 Oxford Circus

Drink, Shop & Do
9 Caledonian Road, N1 9DX
☎ 0203 343 9138
www.drinkshopdo.com
🚇 King's Cross

Duck Tours
55 York Road, SE1 7NJ
☎ 020 7928 3132
www.londonducktours.co.uk
Departure Point: Duck Stop,
Chicheley Street
London, SE1 7PY
🚇 Waterloo

The Fan Museum
12 Crooms Hill, SE10 8ER
☎ 020 8305 1441
www.thefanmuseum.org.uk

Foyles
113–119 Charing Cross Road, WC2H 0EB
☎ 020 7437 5660
www.foyles.co.uk
⊖ Tottenham Court Road or Leicester Square

The Gherkin
30 St Mary Axe, EC3A 8BF
www.30stmaryaxe.co.uk
⊖ Aldgate or Liverpool Street

The Ghost Bus Tours
(Departing from outside the Grand Hotel)
Northumberland Avenue,
off Trafalgar Square, WC2N 5BY
☎ 0844 5678 666
www.theghostbustours.com
⊖ Charing Cross or Embankment

Greenwich Market
Greenwich Church Street, SE10 9HZ
☎ 020 8858 8997
www.shopgreenwich.co.uk
⊖ Greenwich (overground)

Greenwich Park
Charlton Way, SE10 8QY
☎ 0300 061 2380
DLR Cutty Sark (DLR) or
⊖ Greenwich (overground)

Hamleys
188–196 Regent Street, W1B 5BT
☎ 0871 704 1977
www.hamleys.com
⊖ Oxford Circus or Piccadilly Circus

Hampstead Heath Lido
Parliament Hill Fields,
Gordon House Road, NW5 1LP
☎ 020 7485 3873
⊖ Hampstead Heath

Hampton Court and Maze
Hampton Court, Surrey, KT8 9AU
☎ 0844 482 7777
www.hrp.org.uk/hamptoncourtpalace
⊖ Hampton Court (overground)

Harrods
87–135 Brompton Road, SW1X 7XL
☎ 020 7730 1234
www.harrods.com
⊖ Knightsbridge

HMS Belfast
Morgan's Lane, Tooley Street, SE1 2JH
☎ 020 7940 6300
www.iwm.org.uk/visits/hms-belfast
⊖ London Bridge

The Horniman Museum
100 London Rd, Forest Hill, SE23 3PQ
☎ 020 8699 1872
www.horniman.ac.uk
⊖ Forest Hill (overground)

Holland Park
Ilchester Place, W8 6LU
☎ 020 7361 3003
⊖ Holland Park

Hyde Park
W2 2UH
☎ 0300 061 2000
⊖ Hyde Park Corner or Lancaster Gate

Hyde Park Riding Stables
63 Bathurst Mews, W2 2SB
☎ 020 7723 2813
www.hydeparkstables.com
⊖ Lancaster Gate

The Illustration Cupboard
22 Bury Street, SW1Y 6AL
☎ 020 7976 1727
www.illustrationcupboard.com
⊖ Green Park

Jason's Trip (Canal Boat Ride)
Opposite 42 Blomfield Road, W9 2PF
www.jasons.co.uk
⊖ Warwick Avenue

Kensington Palace
Kensington Palace State Apartments,
Kensington Gardens, W8 4PX
☎ 0844 482 7777
www.hrp.org.uk/kensingtonpalace
⊖ High Street Kensington

Kew Gardens
Kew Road, Richmond, Surrey, TW9 3AB
☎ 020 8332 5655.
www.kew.org
⊖ Kew Gardens

Leicester Square
WC2H 7BP
⊖ Leicester Square or Piccadilly Circus

Liberty
210-220 Regent Street, W1B 5AH
(Main entrance is on Great
Marlborough Street)
☎ 020 7734 1234
www.liberty.co.uk
⊖ Oxford Circus

London Bead Shop
24 Earlham Street, WC2H 9LN
☎ 020 7379 9214
www.londonbeadshop.co.uk
⊖ Covent Garden or Leicester Square

The London Bicycle Tour Company
1a Gabriel's Wharf, SE1 9PP
☎ 020 7928 6838
www.londonbicycle.com
⊖ Nearest underground: Waterloo

London Brass Rubbing Centre
6 St Martin's Place, Trafalgar Square,
WC2N 4NJ
☎ 020 7766 1122
www.smitf.org
⊖ Charing Cross

London Dungeon
28–34 Tooley Street, SE1 2SZ
☎ 020 7403 7221
www.thelondondungeon.co.uk
⊖ London Bridge

The London Eye
County Hall, SE1 7PB
☎ 0870 990 8883
www.londoneye.com
⊖ Waterloo

London Film Museum
County Hall, Westminster Bridge Road,
SE1 7PB
☎ 020 7202 7040
www.londonfilmmuseum.com
⊖ Westminster or Waterloo

London Transport Museum
Covent Garden Piazza, WC2E 7BB
☎ 020 7379 6344
www.ltmuseum.co.uk
⊖ Covent Garden

London Walks
☎ 020 7624 3978
www.walks.com

Address

London Waterbus Company

Brownings Pool (Warwick Avenue side), W9
and off Chalk Farm Road, Camden, NW1

☎ 020 7482 2550

www.londonwaterbus.com

⊖ Warwick Avenue / Camden Town

London Wetlands

Queen Elizabeth's Walk, Barnes,
SW13 9WT

☎ 020 8409 4400

www.wwt.org.uk/london

⊖ Hammersmith

London Zoo

Regent's Park, NW1 4RY

☎ 0844 225 1826

www.zsl.org

⊖ Regent's Park or Camden Town

Madame Tussauds

Marylebone Road, NW1 5LR

☎ 0871 894 3000

www.madametussauds.com/london

⊖ Baker Street

Magma

16 Earlham Street, WC2H 9LD

☎ 020 7240 7571

www.mymagma.com

⊖ Covent Garden or Leicester Square

Monument

Monument Street, EC3R 8AH

☎ 020 7626 2717

www.themonument.info

⊖ Monument

Mudchute Park and Farm

Pier Street, E14 3HP

☎ 020 7515 5901

www.mudchute.org

DLR Mudchute (DLR) or Crossharbour (DLR)

Museum of Brands, Packaging and Advertising

2 Colville Mews, Lonsdale Road, W11 2AR

☎ 020 7908 0880

www.museumofbrands.com

⊖ Notting Hill Gate

Museum of Childhood

Cambridge Heath Road, E2 9PA

☎ 020 8983 5200

www.vam.ac.uk/moc

⊖ Bethnal Green

Museum of London

150 London Wall, EC2Y 5HN

☎ 020 7001 9844

www.museumoflondon.org.uk

⊖ Barbican or St Paul's

Namco

County Hall, Westminster Bridge Road,
SE1 7PB

☎ 020 7967 1066

www.namcofunscape.com/london

⊖ Waterloo or Westminster

National Gallery

Trafalgar Square, WC2N 5DN

☎ 020 7747 2885

www.nationalgallery.org.uk

⊖ Charing Cross

National Portrait Gallery

St Martin's Place, WC2H 0HE

☎ 020 7306 0055

www.npg.org.uk

⊖ Charing Cross

Natural History Museum

Cromwell Road, SW7 5BD

☎ 020 7942 5000

www.nhm.ac.uk

⊖ South Kensington

Official London Theatre

Tickets are only available
through the website.
www.officiallondontheatre.co.uk

The Old Curiosity Shop

13–14 Portsmouth Street, WC2A 2ES
☎ 020 7405 9891
www.curiosityuk.com
⊖ Holborn

Original London Sightseeing Tour Ltd

17-19 Cockspur Street, SW1Y 5BL
☎ 020 8877 1722
www.theoriginaltour.com

Paperchase

213–215 Tottenham Court Road,
W1T 7PS
☎ 020 7467 6200
www.paperchase.co.uk
⊖ Goodge Street

Petticoat Lane

Middlesex Street, E1 7EX
⊖ Aldgate or Liverpool Street

Piccadilly Circus

W1J 9HS
⊖ Piccadilly Circus

Playlounge

19 Beak Street, W1F 9RP
☎ 020 7287 7073
www.playlounge.co.uk
⊖ Oxford Circus or Piccadilly Circus

Portobello Market

Portobello Road, W11 1LU
www.portobellomarketlondon.com
⊖ Notting Hill Gate or Ladbroke Grove

Puppet Theatre Barge

Find the barge opposite:
35 Blomfield Road, W9 2PF
☎ 020 7249 6876
www.puppetbarge.com
⊖ Warwick Avenue

Qu'tse

55–57 Charing Cross Road, WC2H 0NE
www.qutse.com
⊖ Leicester Square

Regent's Park

NW1 4NR
www.royalparks.gov.uk/The_Regent_Park.aspx
⊖ Regent's Park or Baker Street

Richmond Park

Surrey, TW10 5HS
www.royalparks.gov.uk/Richmond_Park.aspx
⊖ Richmond

Ripley's Believe It Or Not

The London Pavilion,
1 Piccadilly Circus, W1J 0DA
☎ 020 3238 0022
www.ripleyslondon.com
⊖ Piccadilly Circus

Royal Mews

Buckingham Palace Road, SW1W 1QH
☎ 020 7766 7302
www.royalcollection.org.uk
⊖ Victoria

The Royal National Theatre

South Bank, SE1 9PX
☎ 020 7452 3400
www.nationaltheatre.org.uk
⊖ Waterloo

Address

Royal Observatory

Blackheath Avenue, SE10 8XJ

☎ 020 8312 6565

www.nmm.ac.uk

DLR Cutty Sark (DLR) or
⊖ Greenwich (overground)

The Royal Opera House & Ballet

Bow Street, Covent Garden, WC2E 9DD

☎ 020 7304 4000

www.roh.org.uk

⊖ Covent Garden

Sealife London Aquarium

County Hall, SE1 7PB

☎ 0871 663 1678

www.visitsealife.com/london

⊖ Waterloo or Westminster

Science Museum

Exhibition Road, SW7 2DD

☎ 020 7942 4000

www.sciencemuseum.org.uk

⊖ South Kensington

Selfridges

400 Oxford Street, W1A 1AB

☎ 0800 123 400

www.selfridges.com

⊖ Bond Street or Marble Arch

Serpentine Lido

Hyde Park, W2 3XA

☎ 020 7706 3422

⊖ Lancaster Gate or Hyde Park Corner

Shakespeare's Globe

21 New Globe Walk, Bankside, SE1 9DT

☎ 020 7902 1400

www.shakespearesglobe.com

⊖ London Bridge or Mansion House

Sherlock Holmes Museum

221b Baker Street, NW1 6XE

☎ 020 7224 3688

www.sherlock-holmes.co.uk

⊖ Baker Street

Skating Heaven

Newham Leisure Centre,
281 Prince Regent Lane, E13 8SD

☎ 020 7511 4477

www.skatingheaven.com

⊖ Plaistow

St James's Park

SW1A 2BJ

www.royalparks-gov-uk

⊖ St James's Park or Charing Cross

St Paul's Cathedral

The Chapter House
St Paul's Churchyard
London, EC4M 8AD

☎ 020 7246 8348

www.stpauls.co.uk

⊖ St Paul's

Tatty Devine

44 Monmouth Street, WC2H 9EP

☎ 020 7836 2685

www.tattydevine.com

⊖ Covent Garden or Leicester Square

Tate Modern

Bankside, SE1 9TG

☎ 020 7887 8888

www.tate.org.uk/modern

⊖ Southwark

Thames River Service

Westminster Pier, SW1A 2JH

☎ 020 7930 4097

www.thamesriverservices.co.uk

Tokyo Toys
13 Coventry Street, W1D 7DH
☎ 020 3370 8916
www.tokyotoys.com
⊖ Piccadilly Circus

Topshop
216 Oxford Street, W1D 1LA
☎ 0844 8487 487
www.topshop.com
⊖ Oxford Circus

Tower Bridge
Tower Bridge Road, SE1 2UP
☎ 020 7403 3761
www.towerbridge.org.uk
⊖ Tower Hill or London Bridge

Tower of London
Tower Hill, EC3N 4AB
☎ 0844 482 7777
www.hrp.org.uk/toweroflondon
⊖ Tower Hill

Tooting Bec Lido
Tooting Bec Road, SW16 1RU
☎ 020 8871 7198
⊖ Tooting Bec

Trafalgar Square
WC2 5DN
⊖ Charing Cross

Unicorn Theatre
147 Tooley Street, SE1 2HZ
☎ 020 7645 0560
www.unicorntheatre.com
⊖ London Bridge or Tower Hill

V&A
Cromwell Road, SW7 2RL
☎ 020 7942 2000
www.vam.ac.uk
⊖ South Kensington

The Vault, Hard Rock Cafe
150 Old Park Lane, W1K 1QZ
☎ 020 7629 0382
www.hardrock.com/london
⊖ Hyde Park Corner

VV Rouleaux
261 Pavilion Road, SW1X 0BP
☎ 020 7730 3125
www.vvrouleaux.com
⊖ Sloane Square

Warner Bros Studio Tour
South Way, Leavesden,
Hertfordshire, WD25 7LR
☎ 0845 840 900
www.wbstudiotour.co.uk
⊖ Watford (overground)

Wembley Stadium
Empire Way, HA9 0WS
☎ 0844 800 2755
www.wembleystadium.com/tours
⊖ Wembley Park or Wembley Central

Westminster Abbey
Broad Sanctuary, SW1P 3PA
☎ 020 7222 5152
www.westminster-abbey.org
⊖ Westminster

**Wimbledon/All England
Lawn Tennis Club**
Church Road, Wimbledon, SW19 5AE
☎ 020 8946 6131
www.wimbledon.com/visiting/tours
⊖ Wimbledon or Wimbledon Park

Index

Address

139

Picture Credits:

Page 12 © London Duck Tours ltd, page 45 © Agencyby/Dreamstime.com, page 46 © Arim44/Dreamstime.com, page 48 © Prestong/Dreamstime.com, page 53 © Phil Ashley courtesy of St Martin-in-the-Fields, page 61 © Cartoon Museum, p70 © bikeworldtravel/bigstock.com p74 © Illustration Cupboard p79 © elvisvaughn/bigstock.com, p80 © Joselito Briones/iStock.com, p98 © Will Jarvis, p102 © Chris Price/iStock.com

All other images used under license from Shutterstock.

The publishers thank the following for their kind co-operation with the photography involved in this book: London Duck Tours, St Martin-In-The-Fields, the Illustration Cupboard and the Cartoon Museum.

Every effort has been made to trace the copyright holders of material in this book and to ensure the accuracy of the factual information included. If any rights have been omitted, or any factual errors have occurred, the publishers offer to rectify in a future edition, following notification.